KIP AND SHADOW

DAVID PIETRANDREA

"The body is the ponderable, material, terrestrial thing, endowed with a shadow...."

— M. M. Pattison Muir, The Story of Alchemy and the Beginnings of Chemistry

London, 1881

1

The calls and screams of animals came from every cage. It was a primal sound, pure and frightening. Kip hadn't expected this when he'd taken the job. He hadn't expected to feel the tug of anxiety as it tried to overwhelm him.

They waited in the ticket booth at the entrance to the London Zoo. Its thin wooden panels kept out the chill of the night air. Kip's green satchel sat on the table in front of him, his life's work inside it. Every tonic, tincture, and powder; all the tools of his craft tucked into neat compartments. He fiddled with them as they waited.

The small hut was a museum of newspaper clippings. They were pinned to the walls showing the parade of exotic animals that had passed through the gates.

The striped tiger from Bengal.

The pygmy marmoset.

A speckled aardwolf.

Most had been temporary residents, only here long enough to be gawked at before taken somewhere else.

Others had died in their cages, not equipped for the noise and smog and stresses of London.

The anxiety wouldn't go away.

He ran his fingers through his auburn hair and then pulled at his shirt, as if ordering himself would order his mind. He'd dressed up for the job, wearing a deep red tie, tucked into a plain vest with ebony buttons. His sleeves were rolled up, the trace of chemicals and powders on his hands and arms. But dressing for the part had done nothing to calm him.

His companion, Shadow, didn't seem to share his worries.

Shadow's blue-orb eyes appeared and disappeared as he turned his head, taking in the sounds of the zoo; the screech of a bird, the scream of gibbon. Kip had never seen his friend look so alert. He was especially cat-like tonight as his small, spectral form absorbed the moonlight, carving a darker shade in the night. A misty tail snaked behind him like a question mark. It was matched by a tuft of darkness on his head in place of ears. He crouched on all-fours, his compact body loaded like a spring.

He turned his flat face to Kip.

"Shadow always wanted to go to the zoo."

"I know," Kip said. "It's better in the daytime. They have popcorn."

Kip heard a sharp whistle from Constable Hewitt, two quick bursts of sound that cut through the air.

"He's coming back. Should we go out to meet him?"

Shadow nodded. He breathed on the surface of a metal flask left on the table, watching his reflection appear and disappear.

They pushed open the door and stepped outside.

Massive roman columns stretched overhead and moved out in a half circle, connecting to the first cages of the park. Hundreds of rod-iron stakes made tiny worlds for every bit of exotica and all the sounds that came with it.

Kip remembered the zoo from his childhood. He could see the map of it spreading out in front of him. He'd spent summers watching animals perform on the stage at the center of the park, or the violence of a Punch and Judy show as actors savaged their puppets. Two pools of water surrounded the stage, making a small island at the heart of the zoo.

A large fire pit stood a few feet away, an empty copper disc inviting flames. Kip imagined it burning, the flames dancing, the crackling mingling with the sounds of animals. It was a primitive continent here in the center of London.

He saw smoke rising from chimney tops, Londoners tucked in for the night, forgetting they were so close to an alien world. Somewhere, just over those chimneys, was his home, Alchemy House. He could almost see its low tower and shingled rooftop. He longed for it, to be wrapped in its walls; to close the door on the world.

Footsteps interrupted his thoughts. Constable Raleigh Hewitt approached, breathing heavily, his cheeks flushed. His eyes darted in all directions as if he expected an attack at any moment. Scotland Yard contacted Kip only when it was absolutely necessary. There was a tension between law enforcement and the Great Houses of London. Alchemy House was no exception.

The constable spoke in a whisper.

"I checked each cage. Something's been at them. You can see the claw marks in the door and what looks like bite marks on the metal. What could leave such marks, I don't know."

"Canis Lupus." Kip said. "The western gray wolf of North America."

The constable laughed nervously. "Surely not, Master Kip. The zoo's only specimen died three weeks ago."

"And that's exactly when the killing of other animals began. There's been no evidence of break-ins, just some fierce thing slaughtering animals without a trace."

Hewitt paused, processing this new theory. He pulled a chestnut pipe from his jacket and filled the bowl with tobacco. Kip caught the scent of cherry.

"Chief Sergeant Axton was skeptical of your claims, but wanted to try anything. He thought the master of Alchemy House could surely help."

Still skeptical, Kip thought. *That's why we're here at night, under the cover of darkness.*

"How's it all work?" The constable asked, speaking around his pipe as he cupped his hands over it. The flare of a match lit his face.

Kip wanted to impress this man and his superior. He wanted to show them the power of his art form. But he'd never been a showman. His explanations always sounded too rehearsed and labored.

"As alchemists we believe the material world can be distilled down to base elements, all matter wants to be refined to its most basic form. The wolf would be no different. It's left an imprint of itself on this world, even if its form has been corrupted.

"I believe the base elements that comprised it are still present, having taken another form. I believe we can call back those base elements. If we can reconstitute them we may be able to 'summon' a pale reflection of the wolf."

Pale, Kip thought. No matter how sophisticated his arts, that's all it would be.

He watched Hewitt's eyes move over Shadow as he took in this new information. It was the same reaction for anyone who met him, part seeing and accepting, and part bafflement. It was as if they saw him and were forgetting him at the same time. *It's the same for me*, Kip thought. Shadow fell between reality and dream, something half-remembered.

The constable broke from his daydream.

"You seem quite artful in these processes, for someone so young," He'd been fishing for Kip's age, maybe not willing to commit to someone so young, not wanting to trust his case and career to a boy.

"I'm twenty, long past my apprenticeship. Long enough to attain the appropriate knowledge. I'm also the Master of Alchemy House."

The roar of a lion cut through the air.

"Hell's teeth," Hewitt hissed. "You'd think we were in the jungle."

"The jungle's come to us."

"So what do you propose?"

"I think the wolf is killing other animals." Hewitt made to interrupt him again, but Kip held up a hand. "I think it's found a way back to this plane, chemically. Some form of it is stuck here. I intend to call it back now and then purify it."

"Purify it?"

"Break its bond to this world."

Hewitt sighed. "You know best, I'm sure. Best get on with it, if you're getting on."

Kip nodded, and saw Shadow nod in unison out of the

corner of his eye. He then reached for the green satchel at his feet, cracking it open and smelling the familiar fragrance of aged leather. He reached into it and pulled out two small glass vials and a pewter plate.

He stood, pulling down the edge of his vest, and walked to the fire pit. It seemed like the right spot for such a ritual. He set the plate in the center and emptied the contents of one of the vials onto it. It looked like a bit of crushed coal with the glint of small blue particles mixed in.

"Two drams of borax and one of antimony, to agitate the connection between our world and the next."

Shadow padded over and rose on his hind legs, his paws on the lip of the disc. The glow from his eyes turned the copper blue.

Kip pulled the cork from the second vial with a sharp *pop*, and poured a viscous liquid onto the plate. A sharp blaze of green flared as the two elements touched. A curling ribbon of smoke rose into the air. It flitted away, hurrying up one of the columns and disappearing into the night sky. Hewitt approached cautiously as Kip worked.

"As you know, Constable, there's no known process for bringing something dead back to life, but we can hope to make contact through the veil.

"A warning though, the experience can be...disruptive. We don't know what aspects of the wolf will emerge. A soul can be like a diamond, many facets anchoring it together. Break one and the entire stone can come apart. Who knows what will remain."

Constable Hewitt nodded dutifully, staring into the glowing embers on the plate. A steady stream of smoke rose from his pipe.

"Ready?" Kip asked, turning to his spectral friend.

"Sure," Shadow purred with his child-like voice. He fidgeted with a medal he'd pinned to his chest, something he'd found in a drawer in Alchemy House. It had a bit of red and white-striped fabric that led to a golden disc. He looked at Kip, his lips parting for a moment, revealing his blueish, rounded teeth.

"Very well," Hewitt said. He reached into another pocket and pulled out a folded handkerchief. Carefully unfolding it, he handed the contents to Kip.

It was a tuft of the wolf's hair, a neat bundle of black and gray. Kip took it in both hands and held it over the plate. He thought he felt a tug as if the fur were drawn to the fire. He let it fall into the plate.

Then came the blast.

A sensory explosion, something hidden in the air between them, tugged at the very matter that bound the world together. A loud *crack* followed by the gathering of green light. It hung in the air above the fire pit, thin veins of green knitting together.

Two emerald eyes came into focus above the plate. They were wild, searching back and forth.

For prey.

Kip felt a static charge move through the air. It crawled over his skin, giving him gooseflesh. The smell of sulfur breathed from the center of the pit.

Hewitt backed away.

Smoke turned to light and wrapped itself around the eyes. The green threads knitted together, the light carved shapes in the air. First just a suggestion and then a more solid form. Four paws landed on the copper disc, splayed claws scraped the surface. The ghost of bones and muscles wound together. It ended with a thick, bristling collar of fur.

The wolf was no longer a theory. It was here, and real, and angry.

Emerald eyes burned. They spoke to Kip.

Why did you summon me here? What right did you have?

The beast howled, its voice echoing as if bouncing between two worlds.

It reared up and then fractured into a dozen pieces, blazing like green fireworks. Explosions moved in a circle around Kip, Shadow, and Hewitt; a spectral threat display that penned them in.

The light flared on their faces, making them look sickly. Hewitt pulled a knife from his belt, its metal a tiny blaze.

"We won't stop it that way!" Kip yelled.

He imagined it lashing out, its teeth on their necks before they could react. He would have to make his own threat display.

Kip reached into his bag and pulled out a handful of tiny paper bundles, each packed with a mixture of his own invention. He threw them to the ground where they exploded with a sharp *snap*. The blast pulsed through every color of the spectrum, tiny explosions ricocheted through the air.

Shadow bounced on his tiny legs and clapped like a child.

As if injured by the explosions, the wolf's splintered form came back together with a *snap*. It let out a piercing yelp, then jumped from the pit. It was a cloud of green now as it moved away from them like a ghost, speeding down the center alley of the zoo. Its green light moved out through the mist like a searchlight, disturbing each caged animal it passed.

"Have you seen this before?" Hewitt yelled.

"Yes," Kip said as he thought, *No. Nothing like this.*

Shadow spoke breathlessly.

"It's hunting, Kip. It wants prey. Shadow will be the prey and the bait!"

He laughed and jumped from the stairs before Kip could protest. This was the part Shadow liked, the chase. Kip's friend was coiled action waiting to pounce.

"Lead him to the stage!" Kip yelled.

"Why the stage?" Hewitt asked.

"It has two pools of water on either side and the aviary behind it. I don't think it will want to cross the water. We can trap it there."

There was no time for more talk. They ran into the mist.

It was another world. Shapes moved by like passing ships in a fog. Kip imagined wooden masts and tattered sails. Some magic was at work, shrouding everything in the same in-between world where the wolf lived.

Shadow's voice sounded distant before it faded to nothing.

Kip kept moving forward, reaching one hand out to find the metal bars of a cage. Snatches of Shadow's laughter cut through the atmosphere, sharp bursts of sound, followed by the howls of the wolf. They moved in a circle around him. Distant and then near.

His friend's blue eyes raced towards him, two vibrating orbs. He felt the breeze as Shadow flew by, followed by the hulking shape of the wolf, an invisible force that knocked him out of the way.

Thrown back against the bars of a cage, the cold iron dug into Kip's back. A concussion of sound filled his ears as something slammed against the bars, sent him reeling. He fell to the ground as a massive shape reared up in the darkness. It kicked at the iron with giant, leathery feet.

Kip covered his ears as it trumpeted again, its trunk curled in an S-shape. Flat ears fanned the mist that surrounded it.

African elephants ears are the shape of Africa, he thought madly, his mind offering up some bit of knowledge.

He saw the glint of an eye and the keen intelligence there.

There would be time to ponder all of it later, time to think in the safety of Alchemy House.

He got back on his feet and ran.

Just get to the stage.

The stage was the center point of the zoo, the place everything flowed to. In the daylight it was a place for laughing children and the reveal of new wonders. Poor animals paraded in front of gawking crowds, forced to perform.

In the darkness it looked different. It looked like abandoned ruins, something left by a lost civilization.

The water in the pool was still and black, an amphitheater carved into it.

Stairs went from the amphitheater up to the stage. Behind it was the caged aviary. Its ornate bars twisted into criss-crossing patterns. Darks shapes moved inside it, calling out with shrill voices.

Kip ran up the stairs and onto the stage.

A papier-mâché sea serpent hung above him, suspended by thick ropes. It watched him, its leering mouth open showing white teeth. It was a prop for some children's play, showing them danger in a tamed world. A painted curtain hung to one side, covered with images of wooden ships lost on the sea.

Pulleys and thick ropes hung like gallows from a wooden

scaffold over the stage. Kip climbed a ladder to his right and pulled himself onto the scaffold. It creaked under his weight as it swayed back and forth. He came face to face with the serpent, its mouth gaping and hungry.

Decomposition.

That was the key. He could break apart the wolf's chemical trail, decompose the creature that lingered behind.

He slipped his bag from his back and, reaching into it, found a glass jar sealed with wax. A shimmering liquid moved inside it. He removed the seal and dropped a metal ball into the jar, no bigger than a piece of gunshot. The liquid delighted in touching another element and began to smoke and hiss.

Tools ready, now he needed the subject of his experiment.

Kip brought his fingers to his mouth and gave a sharp whistle. He hoped it would cut through the fog.

Laughter echoed.

Kip pulled his Sulfur Glass from his bag and held it to his eyes. Through the dark window, he could see a new world. The Glass revealed all the invisible markers that humans couldn't see; paths of smell, sound, and hidden auras. They mixed together in the night.

He spotted Shadow's familiar blue trail – coming from the wrong direction. The aviary stood between him and the stage.

His friend went pale, fading out as he met the bars, his body slipping between them. He scrambled over the artificial landscape that filled the cage; dead tree limbs in its center twisting together, making a home for the birds. A dead place to rest their clipped wings.

The wolf crashed into the cage, exploding in green.

Teeth and claws ripped at the bars as they punched through the metal.

Shadow ran along the inside, moving in wide circles as the wolf followed. They were two fireflies in a jar, a spinning whirlwind of light. Birds dashed themselves against the bars as feathers fell to the ground.

"This way, Shadow!" Kip yelled.

Shadow turned and came straight towards Kip. He flew through the opposite side of the cage. The bars passed through his body. He bounded onto the stage and turned to face the wolf, sticking out his blue tongue and wagging it at the beast behind him.

The wolf followed, taking the bait.

Shadow went pale again and fell through the stage and out of sight, just as the wolf reached him. It clawed at the empty spot where its prey had been and then raised its head to howl.

The sound never passed its lips as it spied Kip above him. Their eyes locked.

The wolf's hypnotic green eyes, so filled with rage, and something deeper. An endless whirlpool that Kip could fall into.

He struggled to tear himself away. Taking a deep breath, he dropped another sphere into the mason jar.

Expansion.

The liquid exploded upward, a torrent of silver. It arced overhead and then fell straight down onto the beast. The wolf craned its neck to see its attacker as holes carved into its body like acid. The liquid released whatever material remained in this world.

The wolf howled, half in anger and half in pain. There was a universe inside its mouth, a black hole that bent everything towards it. Kip felt reality shift, felt himself tip off the scaffold, in danger of falling straight into it.

A hole in Alchemy House exhibits the same pull, Kip thought *The thing I made, the secret that's waiting for me.*

He clutched the scaffold tighter and shook his head, trying to clear his mind.

The echoed screams rose from below. They came in waves like the peals of a bell.

"I'm sorry," Kip said. He wanted to say it again and again. He watched the thing scream, shredding itself. It bit at its own limbs, pulling away glowing chunks of green. Its eyes burned white. It turned in furious circles as its body evaporated. Shocks of lightning etched the air as they blended with the falling liquid.

Standing stock-still, Shadow watched from the base of the stairs, his laughter silenced.

Smoke rose from the stage. Its choking sulfur filled Kip's lungs and brought tears to his eyes. The green vapor wreathed the head of the papier-mâché serpent, then ignited the paper. The fire spread over it in a flash. Kip pushed away from it as heat swept over the scaffold.

A final howl below rose from the stage and into the sky above.

Then silence.

The last of the green mist trailed off into the night.

Kip dropped down to the stage. Scorch marks and deep cuts ruined its surface. The serpent sputtered above them as it burned down to a wire frame before extinguishing.

Shadow padded up the stairs to meet Kip. He stared at him, his blue eyes lingering for too long.

"What are you thinking, Shadow?" Kip asked quietly.

"Shadow doesn't know. It's sad. The zoo feels lonely and cold."

"Yes, it does."

"Is this what the zoo's always like?"

"Not usually. In the daytime they have popcorn."

They stood in front of the aviary. Its bent and broken bars pushed out like an exploded ribcage. They stepped inside and looked up at the ornate frame that cut through the stars above. The cage should have been filled with sound. Kip waited to hear the panicked calls of kingfishers, peacocks, and lorikeets. But there was only silence.

Shadow clung to Kip's pant leg, peering out.

"It killed the birds."

It had. Feathers littered the ground; a collage of patterns and colors. Beyond that, Kip didn't want to see.

Bodies ripped open, necks twisted, and eyes staring.

Footfalls on the steps behind them interrupted the pervasive silence. Constable Hewitt ran up, all puffed-up excitement.

"Master Kip, I've never seen anything like it! Well done, well done, I say!"

He stopped cold as he took in the carnage. He slowly pulled his cap from his head.

"Hell's teeth."

2

The two walked in silence. The streets of London were abandoned, the calm of night left nothing but shadows. A fog closed in on them, the echo of their feet on the cobblestones trapped in its atmosphere.

Shadow padded along beside Kip on all-fours. He'd stop on occasion, standing on his hind legs, as he craned his neck to see some point of interest, whether it was the burning flame of a street lamp or the empty storefront of a sweets shop, bereft of pastries. The creature's head was down now, his behavior unusually focused. His blue-orb eyes projected light onto the wet cobblestones.

"Kip told Constable Hewitt, 'there's no known process for bringing the dead back to life.' What did he mean?"

Kip felt drained by the question, drained by the day itself, finding it remarkable that he'd had the strength to make it around the bend of the clock once more.

"What did I mean?" Kip repeated. "Just what I said. There's no known process, alchemic or otherwise. That was a chemical echo of the wolf, nothing more."

"But Kip hopes there is a process, alchemic or otherwise? Kip's trying to find it?"

Kip loved Shadow, but was less fond of his constant inquisitiveness. He could turn any conversation into a string of questions, each one rattled off with dazzling speed.

"There are things the Constable Hewitts of this world don't need to know, Shadow, things that are mine."

"But what Kip's doing in the basement of Alchemy House..."

"Is my business."

Shadow seemed less sure, but he fell quiet.

Kip wanted to say more. He hated being curt, even though it came to him so easily these days. Something in him wanted to apologize immediately, and something else wanted to make it worse; to sneer and insult and wound.

He sighed, his breath visible in the cool air.

"I'm sorry, Shadow."

"Hmm?"

The spectral creature had lost interest once again. He jumped onto the curb, prancing from cobblestone to cobblestone while he hummed mindlessly.

Kip watched him. Shadow was the curiosity that he'd brought into this world. Like so much of his life now, the memories were hazy. Things that should have been solid were soft. He tried to focus on the exact moment but it was always two steps ahead, turning a corner. It was what he'd done in the basement. Shadow had come from that, hadn't he? Many things had come from that.

And more will come still, he thought.

Where did you come from, little one?

I think you know, a voice answered. It was the basement voice and it was waiting for him.

They descended a curving stone staircase. It widened at the bottom and opened up into a large courtyard – Potter's Market, buttoned up for the night. The purveyors and barkers had gone home, having sold their wares for another day. Kip could practically see the energy still buzzing there, he knew it so well.

They passed the Three Nymphs Fountain and he let out a small gasp as memory punched through the world of the present. Shadow looked up at him, his eyes unreadable.

The dribble of water from the statue in the center coated the stone with a glassy sheen. In the daylight it would return to full force, catching the sunlight and splintering it into a thousand drops.

So much blood. There had been so much blood.

Did Shadow know what had happened here? Could the creature divine it somehow? Kip thought anyone who looked at him could read his heart now. He wore it outside his chest.

Let the Three Nymphs be, he thought. *Let them rest. No need to drag their secrets into the light.*

They turned the corner onto Aldgate Street, and saw the Thames in the far distance, jet-black now in the fading light. It looked like a void at the end of the world. The lamps that lined the street were dimmed to a flicker, some already extinguished.

"Hello, Magic Boy," a voice slurred, cutting the silence.

Kip turned to follow the greeting. A man stood under a lamppost on the corner, half in light and half in shadow. He was wrapped in a decaying trench coat, long separated from its buttons. It hung in tatters around his legs. His hair and beard were a wild mess of black and gray that looked more like fur than hair. The man clutched a stained clay jug in his thick hand, held close to him as if for protection. Kip shuddered to think what putrid mixture swirled in its depths.

"It's not magic, it's alchemy, Ragman," Kip answered.

"True enough, young sir, true enough. Heaven forfend we mistake the two. I know incantations myself. I have a practiced hand." He waved one shaking palm over his jug, his fingers contorting in the air.

"How goes your tenancy of Alchemy House? So many rooms all to yourself."

Kip had little patience for Ragman tonight. He had been a near-permanent fixture on Aldgate Street, never straying too far from the parade of daily traffic and the chance for donations. Kip had given his share over the past year.

But once Ragman knew Kip's profession, something had changed. He'd yammered on about gold, and all the alchemic myths he'd heard in his lifetime. His conversations seemed like prying now instead of pleasantries.

"Can you turn a poor man's lead into gold, son?" This was his usual strain of conversation now. The glint in his eye seemed dangerous, some hidden depth revealed.

"Why the lamentation, boy?"

"What lamentation?"

Shadow busied himself peeking into the overturned top hat that Ragman used for collection, his paws resting on the tattered brim.

"I can sense the sorrow on you, I can," the beggar said. "It clings to you, clings to every inch of you."

Kip bristled but said nothing. He reached into his pocket and pulled out a single sixpence, and tossed it into the hat. He heard it hit the felt bottom instead of the clink of metal on metal.

"Slow day," he said. "Let's go, Shadow."

Kip turned and continued down the street.

Shadow stayed behind for a moment, still peering into the battered hat as if it held some secret. He removed the medal from his chest, gave it a final appreciative look, and placed it in the hat.

"Ragman keep this. Shadow's got more," he said cheerfully, then politely said goodbye as he pattered away, catching up with Kip.

Ragman seemed not to notice the gesture, his eyes still fixed on Kip as he walked away.

"You've got a heart of gold, boy! A heart of gold!"

3

The low tower of Alchemy House crested over the surrounding buildings, armored in dark red shingles that moved in a spiraling pattern up the tower, past a round window and to the top of the spire. Four windows at the top looked out under a pointed black-shingled roof.

It cut an imposing form against the deep blue sky, dotted with stars.

Kip always imagined the tower was leaning or twisting somehow, as if it changed with the seasons or on some whim. But when he looked directly at it, it seemed straight again.

Of the four windows at the top of the tower, one was laced with stained glass, colored panes of red and black that formed the symbol of the Alchemists. Moonlight shot through the tower and illuminated it like a lighthouse on some windswept coastline. Alchemy House always called him home.

Shadow jumped the four steps to the front door and

pushed it open.

"Home again," he tittered as he padded inside.

Stillness.

Few things could be as silent as Alchemy House once it was tucked in for the night. The walls shielded it from the outside world, dampening any sound in an uncanny way. Even the clatter of a passing hansom cab failed to penetrate it. Kip had often looked down on the street below and wondered how there could be such silence when the world moved with such tremendous speed below.

But not now. Empty streets and a locked door.

Stillness.

It hadn't always been this way.

In centuries past the house had been full of people, everyone working towards a common purpose.

New ideas hotly debated. New people inducted. Old masters retired. Traditions observed.

It had been that way for centuries. Not anymore.

The shine had worn off of magic and alchemy, replaced by a city on the brink of a new modern age. People embraced the changes around them that raised taller buildings and promised brighter futures. Fewer people wanted to study alchemy, and the Academy had made adjustments accordingly, limiting the number of alchemists and magicians throughout Great Britain until Kip was the only one.

Kip wasn't bitter. It was the way of the world. It was always moving on. But it had left him here, alone, in a house with just memories.

Stillness.

It was exactly what Kip waited for, dreamed of, since the moment he woke that morning. And here it was.

Shadow mewled lazily by the fire for an hour, talking about wolves and spirits and his ideal seven-course meal, then said goodnight, pattering up to the second floor. In the process of finding the most ideal sleeping arrangement, he busied himself with sampling every option. It varied every day. One night he slept on a bookshelf, the works of Aristotle for a pillow. Another night he found an appealing collection of blankets that begged to be sat upon.

And on some nights...

On some nights, Shadow rested on the network of dark tree limbs that filled the house.

Kip looked at them now. Ashen branches interrupted the timbered ceiling, pushing boards aside or cracking them. Some grew from the walls and a few from the floor, thick arms of wood that thinned to grasping fingers. Leaves budded from them; waxy gray-green things that moved in a breeze only they felt.

Despite the strange beauty of it, Kip shuddered. The wolf reared up in his mind again, and the void of its eyes. It was so deep.

I brought this forth, he thought. *I'm transforming Alchemy House with my mind, slowly but surely.*

It seemed impossible, especially to someone trained in such a precise and rational craft, but here was the proof growing above him. He wondered how much the branches would grow and imagined them slowly wrapping the house and everything in it into a timber cocoon.

I brought this forth.

Kip gazed into the hearth, watching the flames perform

their ballet as they blazed and crackled. He looked at the painting above the mantel.

Enos.

The painting was a monument; a young man locked in amber. The eyes stared out at Kip, illuminated by the soft glow from the hearth. The painting could be a comfort or a rock to be dashed against. It responded to his mood, all without magic of any kind.

Or was it a deeper magic?

In his world of potions and elements, controlled experiments and breathless results, the painting held some real magic that Kip couldn't quantify.

The young man in the painting watched him. His black hair, usually so wild, was neatly combed. A thin and perfect line of pink captured his smile. But, no amount of skill could have captured his green eyes and the glint that ignited there. It would have been foolish to try.

It had been one year since Enos had died, one year to the day. Kip shunned every calendar in the house, afraid to call out a day with such heavy memory. But the memories came regardless.

He remembered waking that morning to the tangle of their limbs, the thin sheet half-off the bed, their body heat keeping them warm as the sun streamed in. Particles of dust caught in the light like woodland sprites come for a visit. They danced around the bed, finding their own patterns of flight in the air.

Kip and Enos dressed and went out into the world. The bustle around them could move at the pace it liked, but for them the time passed deliciously slow. They cut through it, carving their own way as the sights and sounds of the world filled their senses. It was almost too much to see and hear, a kind of bewilderment.

They made their way, as they always did, to Potter's Market. They sampled fruits from the Orient, their hands brushing together as they reached for a spiky orange delicacy and listened to the fruit-seller explain its origin in a language they didn't understand.

They tried on hats and laughed far too loud; bowlers, toppers, and squires.

Kip bought eight ounces of turmeric, its earthy smell filling his nose. Enos bought a few strips of balsam wood for a model ship he was working on, remarking on what a mighty mast it would make.

They'd visited Cobble and Crane's Curiosity Shop and marveled at items that seemed too absurd to exist, the old shopkeeper keeping a watchful eye on them.

At the edge of the market, always removed from the crowd, sat the Bird Lady. An old woman with a kind face surrounded by the folds of a babushka. She had a cart that held dozens of cages stacked one on top of the other, keeping their balance despite the strange angles and structures they made. Each contained a small bird.

Parakeets, starlings, jackdaws, sparrows; a flurry of color and sound as the bird song became deafening. It should have disturbed, all those discordant voices, but it was pleasing somehow, like an orchestra tuning up before a concert.

Kip always wondered what the full performance would have been.

For a penny you could free one of the birds. It was a cynical transaction, but beautiful nonetheless. Kip and Enos always shared a cage, taking turns between holding it, and opening the small matchstick door.

It was Enos's turn. They'd given the penny to the Bird Lady's assistant, a girl who couldn't have been more than six. Her eyes flashed with delight each time they gave her a penny and it disappeared into a pocket in her dress faster than sight.

Enos picked a Chickadee and read the small paper tag tied to the bars.

The Chickadee is the symbol of 'clarity and purity of soul,' he said, smiling at Kip.

Kip held the cage up, the bird chirping when the sun streamed through the bars. It tested its wings in a flurry, expanding them as far as its prison would allow. Enos lifted the small gate and the bird darted out so quickly it was nearly invisible.

Its black head bobbed and its grey wings fluttered as it rose into an expanse of blue. Up and up it went until it was gone, disappearing over rooftops and obscured by the sun.

Now it was just this room, and this house, and the portrait that stared, and the fire that danced.

Kip reached into his bag on the armchair, shuffling through a collection of vials and small leather pouches.

One pocket held a reliquary.

Kip pulled out a silver bracelet that caught the light. Enos used to wear it constantly. It went everywhere he went. A lock of black hair tied in a bundle with a piece of red string wrapped around the bracelet.

Leave these things here. They'll be safe.

He pulled out a sack made of purple-stained leather and

loosened the tie. Opening it carefully, he caught the smell of the powder, a mix of iron and char.

Kip grabbed a generous handful and dusted his lower body with it. The dust that fell away evaporated before it hit the floor, but he knew it was still there, like water molecules in the air. Dusting off his hands, he stepped forward into the hearth.

The fire roared around him, flames licked at his legs, trying to consume this new fuel but with no luck. The orange flame sparked to blue as it wrapped around him.

He put his palms against the stone back of the hearth and pushed. A gust of air rushed over him; the fire sputtered fitfully. Kip stepped through the hearth into a long hallway that sloped down.

It was low enough that he had to bend his head slightly. Placing a palm on the ceiling, he ran his hand along the surface above as he walked forward. Branches broke out of the stone, the roots of the tree that expanded to the rest of the house.

A wooden staircase loomed ahead. It was a platform looking down on his basement laboratory, two short flights down to a dirt floor. He descended them and felt an odd comfort when his feet touched the earth.

Heavy work tables lined the walls of the room, each station packed with devices and equipment. Various bronze mortars, crucibles, beakers, and burners crowded the tables. A rack overflowed with ingredients of every kind; powders and liquids, bits of metal, and trapped gases. Candles of varying heights cropped up in any available space, melted onto the wood surface.

His short life's work. But all that work had been pushed

aside for a newcomer, something that grew from the earth itself.

A well.

The rough and unfinished stone reminded him of the work of pagans. He thought of standing stones, and cairns, and all the mysterious structures that had sprung up in this world, so common now that people passed them on the way to market without a second glance.

This well was not common; the gaping hole in his basement that leaked a constant chill. It made him sick to look at it, to know he created something not with his talent or ingenuity, but with pure focused desire. What spoke through him to make such a thing possible? What had he manifested with his longing?

He was the master of Alchemy House, after all, not Magic House. There was supposed to be an order to his world. Logical. Precise. Not the unknown realm of dreams and the power of the mages. Kip no longer believed in such things. They had faded from the world like a giant going to sleep.

But here was a giant awake again.

He looked down into the black hole, just as he did every night. It pulled him in, bending his neck with an invisible weight until he thought he would fall. His fingers brushed the rough stone, its texture now mapped to his body. He knew every piece of the well, every sensation it offered. The coldness of the stone. The smell of the air that breathed slowly from the depths, clean and cold like a breeze that comes over a hill in autumn, shaking the leaves and driving out any last bit of summer. Just like a fall chill, it triggered the same emotions.

"Why?" Kip asked, his voice cracking.

And then came a reply.

"Hunger," the ice voice said. The voice that first spoke three months ago, coming to him in a dream. It was the same dream that brought forth the well. Kip sensed its approach, or at least it was easy to think that now. He imagined it coming for him, pushing back layer after layer of the veil between this world and the next.

"Down here there's a hunger, boy."

"Why did you find me?"

"Because there is life and death, and then something in-between. You must know you're not truly alive? You're Kip of the In-between, who seeks out his bed so that he can dream, who prays to Morpheus with each breath. You called to me as a child of the In-between.

"No amount of alchemical tinkering has that power. You can move your elements and rearrange a drop of sand on a beach, but down here, that's where there's true power."

"I'm going to bring him back."

"No one comes back, boy."

"I will divine a method..."

"No."

"Then why did you find me? What was the point?"

"To know you better, to see the world above. I can feel a city move around you. How can you stand its movement, so constant and pitiless? Down here there's room. You could walk for a day without seeing another. You could walk for one hundred days and only see the gray expanse, and the lightning clouds."

A pause. There were many pauses when he communicated with the well, drawn out and peaceful. The voice spoke again.

"What is that pretty glint?"

Kip looked down at his wrist and the bracelet there. It was the twin to Enos's.

"I made two bracelets. They're made of lodestone incased in iron. They're attracted to each other."

He remembered the sensation, the merest tug of the wrist as one bracelet pulled towards the other. It worked from great distances, strong enough that he and Enos could find each other wherever they might be. Kip remembered the subtle gravity, pulling him left here and right there, down this street and up that alleyway.

"Does it still pull at your wrist?"

It did, even now. Kip could feel the other bracelet in his bag upstairs, constantly nagging.

"Yes."

"Tell me one true thing about him so that I may find him down here."

"He liked Boccherini."

"What is that?"

"It's music. Well, it was a person who composed music."

"What else?"

"He pronounced 'cacophony' wrong."

There was the rhythmic, barely audible, drumbeat again. It rose from the well like water, filling the hole and spilling over. Kip swam in the noise, never sure if it occupied his ears or his mind. Either way, it pulled him closer, invited him to look more keenly into the darkness.

"He liked to build ships in bottles."

Another pause.

"Yes," the gravel-voice said. "He's down here. I can smell him. But your description is sparse. Why do you distill things down to such basic elements? Petty likes and dislikes?"

That's what Alchemists do, Kip wanted to say. *We distill and simplify and break apart the elements of the world.* All the same, he felt like a fool, talking about Boccherini and cacophony when there was so much else to say. But if he started, would he be able to stop?

"Why do you come here to think about death?"

"Death scatters the elements of the body, devolving them. If I can follow the process backwards, reclaim the elements, I could bring something back."

"Like the wolf?"

Kip thought of the ghostly horror, the tortured howls that he'd brought back into the world.

"That...that was just an echo of the wolf. Not the real thing. But, in theory—"

The voice pushed on. "And you would do this for Enos?"

I tried, Kip thought. *It doesn't work.*

The well could hear him, penetrating the workings of his mind as it made him remember.

"How did you try?"

Kip thought of the countless experiments. He'd used his little Enos reliquary. Tortured each object to release some essence, something he could hold on to. He'd burned things with fire and acid, broken them, shattered them. All the work had gotten him nothing, nothing but smoke.

Again, the voice in the well seemed to experience this memory with him, always in step with his thoughts.

"Why couldn't you bring him back?"

"Four elements make up all things: earth, wind, water, fire, each with their chemical analog. But tracing the patterns of something... so wonderful, so alive, it might be impossible. You can't reform a shattered crystal. It's too fine. The human body is too complex."

"The boy wants to reverse the process if he can? Follow the footprints back up the trail?"

He could have screamed his answer, but left it at a single, softly-spoken word. "Yes."

"What is the end goal? When all the notes run together, what is the symphony?"

The Soul of All Things, Kip thought.

"And what is that?"

"It's the end of the journey," he said with reverence. "The goal of every Alchemist throughout history, to find the Primal Element, the thing common to all substances. The element that would allow someone to reshape the world."

Cold air swelled from the well, an exhaling of breath; clean and pure but still dead. A vision appeared, some far-away world or forgotten memory. It warbled to life in front of Kip as if viewed through rippled glass; a gray world of towering stones and scattered lights in the sky.

A silhouette sat against the churning horizon, a young man standing still and watching Kip, unkempt raven hair moved by a breeze.

He stretched out his hand to touch this strange offering but it vanished, collapsing to a pinpoint of light before disappearing.

"How perfect," the voice mused, "The Soul of All Things."

The presence seemed to like that, thinking on it for a moment.

"Are other humans like you, so unreachable?"

"I don't know," Kip said.

And then the question that the voice always came back to.

"What does it feel like to be alive?"

Something about the repeated question alarmed him. There was a threat wrapped in it, no matter how politely the voice asked.

"I have to go. It's late."

"No."

Kip started to back away, his fingers slipping from the stone of the well.

"What does blood feel like? Is the body an open wound? Why else does it bleed from the inside?"

Kip placed one foot on the stairs. He glanced up to see the light of the fire, reflecting off the walls of the hallway and catching in the leaves and branches that hung above. Were they growing even now, before his eyes?

"If blood is a liquid, can you drink it? What does it taste like?"

The drumming returned, louder now and more steady. It filled his ears and then his head. Its low rumble felt organic; like an extension of his body.

Boom. Boom. Boom.

Still Kip didn't allow himself to be afraid. He'd built a dam inside himself, walling off all the important bits, protecting them from petty hurts, from anxiety, from fear...

But those drums.

Kip's hand slipped from the railing and fell to his side. His foot came off the stair and rested back on the dirt floor, a small cloud lifted into the air. He suddenly wanted to feel the dirt between his toes, pushing between each digit. He wanted to feel the strange leaves on his face, battering him as he ran through a jungle, straight into the arms of the ashen limbs.

Boom. Boom. Boom.

The voice was at its most silken now, almost a hiss, and

less human-sounding than ever. Kip wondered at the fact that he could even understand it.

"You are organic, I know that now. I can see it. I can see the blush on your face where the blood gathers. There are small blue veins that carry it to the farthest reaches of your body.

"What if you were punctured, would it run like sap from a tree? How much sap could you lose before you had to join me down here? Down here, with your raven-haired Boccherini-lover."

Kip stepped forward. Curse and bother the world behind him, the fragile and impotent world of men, with its achievements measured in the smallest increments. The world moved at a snail's pace, and with equal grace; sludging from small movement to small movement.

This world that killed Enos, crushed him under the wheel of ignorance. Kip thought of his bed and the nights of focused meditation, wishing and wishing until he thought his skull would crack open, wishing that things could be different, that they could go back to what they'd been.

If only his skull *could* crack and bring forth his own Athena; his Enos.

The drumbeat reached a crescendo and hammered all other thoughts from his mind. Only one voice remained in the coming darkness.

"What does it feel like to be alive?"

4

Kip awoke to bird song. It penetrated the layers of his dream, cutting through the darkness with clear sound. He opened his eyes to see swaying branches above him and sunlight breaking through a mesh of leaves.

He'd fallen asleep next to the well again. Kip brought his hand to his face and covered his eyes, massaging his temples. Sleep called him again, offering to drag him back down, but the hard dirt floor said otherwise.

You could stay here, the well offered. The voice itself was silent, never one to come out during the day, but Kip felt its presence.

Stay here.

Kip shifted his body and sat up with a groan. He rolled onto his knees and then used the well as a prop to pull himself up. The bird was still hyperventilating, singing its fool head off. He followed the sound up the stairs and then back through the hearth, the fire long extinguished. Kip pulled the stone panel shut, then stepped over the bed of ash in the fireplace and into the living room.

He heard the clatter of Shadow in the kitchen, no doubt preparing some Shadow-ish breakfast, which usually ended in something burnt and broken crockery. He was about to join Shadow when a knock at the door stopped him.

A timid knock, Kip wondered if he had even heard until it was repeated. He went to the front door and opened it, pulling in a draft of air.

A girl stood on the doorstep. Her silver-white hair hung in her face, nearly hiding blue eyes with dark circles under them. She wore a faded dress that hung loosely on her body. She looked like she was hiding even when standing right in front of him, as if she were in retreat.

Clover Blackmoor, daughter of the master of Magic House; Lord Francis Blackmoor. She was a mute. Kip felt a sudden pain being in her presence as if he too wanted to shrink away. He found it difficult to meet her eyes, which lay flat on her face like two shallow pools. If there was a depth beneath them, it was unknowable.

Her pale hands clutched a letter with a wax seal. She offered the letter to Kip, as if initiating some planned ceremony. He followed her lead, reaching out with both hands and took it. Clover hesitated before letting go, a moment passed before she surrendered the letter, then her hands fell away.

"Thank you," Kip said. "It's Clover, isn't it?"

The girl brought one hand up to the side of Kip's face and held it there. So random was the gesture that Kip didn't know how to react. He stood there, letting her cradle his cheek, feeling the warmth of her palm.

Her eyes flared suddenly, something penetrating the

blue; a splinter of purple light. Her hand flicked up to Kip's head and she snatched a single strand of hair from his scalp.

"Hey!"

He wanted to say more but she had already turned away in a pale whirl, hurrying down the steps, and walking quickly up the street, before disappearing into the bustle of the London morning.

Kip turned the letter in his hands, felt the fineness of the paper, ran his thumb over the wax seal of Magic House – an image of two manticores locked in combat.

It was a rare occasion that he heard from Lord Francis Blackmoor. They were acquaintances due to their positions, but had never been close. There was an iciness to the old man, hidden just below the surface of his charm. Perhaps magic made one aloof.

Letters can wait, he thought, as he slipped it into his vest pocket, and went to the kitchen.

Shadow was there trying to navigate a steaming teapot while not putting down the book he was reading. He spoke without looking up from his work.

"Shadow made ceylon in Brown Betty," he said proudly, gesturing to the teapot, by tilting his head at an odd angle. He seemed endlessly proud of making tea, as if it were more than hot water poured over leaves.

Kip pulled out one of the kitchen chairs and sat in it heavily, upsetting a few stray pawns from the chessboard on the table. One rolled to the table's edge and Kip stopped it with a single finger, letting it rest, nearly teetering over.

"Shadow's reading about human stuff," Shadow said,

gesturing to the spine of his book. His pleasant child-like voice was always so musical, especially in the morning. Kip reached out and grabbed the book.

"The Moonstone by Wilkie Collins. Is it good?"

"Cracking good!" Shadow said, extending a clawed hand, opening and closing his fist, signaling he wanted it back. Kip obliged.

"What's it about?"

"Human stuff..." Shadow mumbled as he buried his face between the pages. His blue eyes cast a soft glow on the words below.

"Do you like 'human stuff'?"

"Yeah, Shadow likes all stuff...well, most stuff."

"Do you like mysterious letters?"

Kip slipped the envelope from his pocket and cut through the seal with a butter knife. A plume of blue dust rose into the air, escaping the folds of the envelope. As the dust spread, it caught the light through the window and shimmered slightly before disappearing. *The theatrics of Magic House*, he thought; *couch all things in mystery*.

Shadow peered over the spine of his book, his interest and short attention span having moved on to the contents of the letter. Kip smiled without looking up. He mimed reading it silently, his eyebrows raising and lowering with each sentence.

"Please," Shadow whispered, now putting the book on the table. "Read it out loud. Read it to Shadow."

"Very well," Kip said.

Spidery letters filled the page, all legibility nearly replaced by style. He read the words aloud.

Master of Alchemy House,

It seems that time speeds ever-on, and that the circle of our world closes in. The Great Houses of London are but a shadow (Shadow smiled here) of what they once were. Perhaps it is the way of things, the future moves with a dizzying speed and the least of us must hold on tightly or be washed away.

Please forgive a ponderous old man. It is due to my rather grim realizations that I extend this invitation. We must celebrate while we can and hold close those that we value, lest they not feel that value in full.

Wishing you a healthier disposition than I, at present, and hoping for your availability this Saturday: 21 April, 7pm. Join me, and guests, for a night of conversation, exquisite food, and perhaps some magic.

Yours truly,

Lord Francis Blackmoor, Magic House

P.S. - You will find the evening's menu enclosed.

Kip lowered the letter to the table. He'd only been to Magic House twice since completing his apprenticeship as an alchemist. He found it to be an unknowable place, mysteries kept from all, save Lord Blackmoor. Secrets hidden beneath a set of ancient rules.

And when had they been set? Nearly with the founding of London itself. Magic House was the first house, shrouded in the mysteries of its time. It had existed in some form or another since before the Romans had invaded Britannia. Kip had always loved the imagery, ancient people harnessing powers they didn't understand.

Shadow seemed to have less thought on the matter.

"Can Shadow go?" he asked.

"I don't see why not. Do you want to go?"

In a flash of movement he disappeared, contracting to almost nothing. The hint of his form rippled along the side of the table, then sprang to life again, inches from Kip's face. The creature looked deep into his eyes.

"Yes."

Kip smiled. "I'm sure you'll charm the party."

Shadow reached for the envelope and pulled out the card with the dinner menu. He scanned it with his blue-orb eyes.

"'Ballotines de Canard à la Cumberland.' What is it?"

"I'm not sure what that is. Duck...something."

"Good though?"

"Probably."

"Does Kip know two peach pits can kill you?" Shadow inquired, dancing to a new topic.

"How do you mean?"

"Two crushed-up peach pits have enough cyanide to kill a man. It's powdered death!"

Kip didn't know that it would only take such a small quantity, but appreciated the random facts that Shadow offered.

His friend sighed.

"Shadow hopes Lord Blackmoor doesn't serve peaches."

5

T*hree luminaries*, that's what Lord Blackmoor had called them.

Three masters of intellectual thought and accomplishment in London, not to be trifled with. Somehow Kip had been thrust into that category, no matter if he had earned it or not. He looked across the sitting room with quiet wonder at the two guests and their host.

Dr. Stephen Fairfield of the Science Academy, a hefty man as solid as a tree trunk. Wherever he planted his feet he gave the appearance that he was meant to be there, carving out his place in the world with each step. He sat now in a high-backed armchair, lighting a chestnut pipe. Kip watched the glow through Fairfield's fingers as he cradled the flame. He coaxed wisps of smoke from the pipe, twisting and spinning towards the ceiling.

Shadow watched silently, the glow from the fireplace danced in his eyes. He preferred to sit at Kip's feet, curled up in a tight ball, his tail wrapped around a chair leg.

Across from Dr. Fairfield sat Amelia Britten, a quiet and mousy woman who constantly moved her hands, as if she were knitting with invisible yarn. She was a reformed Mother Superior and now a noted spiritualist, her position making her something of a celebrity. The whispered gossip, if one had cared to listen, was that she was on call to the Royal Family.

And then Lord Francis Blackmoor himself, Master of Magic House.

No one was more fitted to his position. He inhabited the title of 'Lord' as if he'd had it since birth, growing into it more fully with each year. There was a theatricality about him. Kip saw it in his public appearances and now, in a private setting. His every move was deliberate; graceful gestures flowing into the perfect joke or comment.

He had a long pale face with two dark pinpoint eyes. His black hair rose to fine points on his head, the only thing on his body that wasn't tamed. A shock of white cut through the dark strands, rising from his forehead into a graceful curl.

The 'luminaries' exchanged introductions and pleasantries before the conversation turned to more serious matters.

Lord Blackmoor took a long sip of his aperitif and then spoke.

"You've read the news today, I assume? Parliament thinks they have a right to oversee Magic House."

"I think we're all shocked that you'd be opposed to that," Fairfield said with a smile.

"I don't expect the Science Academy to understand such things. Half your work you do for the state, racing ahead with notions and inventions no matter how dangerous they might be. I, for one, don't think some up-jumped locals should have the right to meddle.

"If they wish to combine the Houses, how long before they whittle them down to nothing? A cut here, a slice there, until we're nothing more than carnival acts. Oversight and then dismantling. Dark House has slipped from their grasp, but Alchemy and Magic House remain."

Dark House.

It was a place of mystery, like an unearthed artifact that had no story around it, no way to find its place in London's history.

Kip had only been a child when Dark House disappeared. It was the sister to Magic House, sitting on the property behind it; a black structure surrounded by trees and protected by a wrought-iron fence. Sharp gables had peeked above the tree-line, eyes of dark glass.

Then it had vanished.

Some said it had a mind of its own. Others said it was controlled in some manner.

But, like everything, the talk died down over time, leaving just an empty lot and the black trees.

Amelia Britten fidgeted as Blackmoor and Fairfield spoke, waiting for the right moment to interject.

"Don't fight, gentlemen. The night is young and there's a new moon. It's a perilous time with Saturn in retrograde."

Blackmoor let the debate drop.

"Is it true you'll be leaving us soon, Amelia? Leaving London?"

She smiled.

"A vacation is long overdue, I'm afraid. I've got a grand-daughter waiting for me in Somerset and need to see some open and green spaces. This city is so close."

"Speaking of, we all heard about *your* little vacation to the zoo, Master Kip." Blackmoor said.

Kip wished he was anywhere but here. The sound of the crackling fire kept trying to interject, popping and sighing as if it could join the conversation. He wished it could.

"It was nothing." he said, finally.

"Surely not!" Fairfield burst. "The paper mentioned a spectral wolf. Surely not nothing! Perhaps you could give us a demonstration?"

"So much talent from one so young," Britten said with a wink. "Yes, a demonstration!"

Kip had brought his green bag, in case Blackmoor requested just such a thing. Seeing the company, he hoped not, preferring to observe instead. He had never been a showman, he'd never charmed a crowd or embellished his abilities. What was the point in being false? Surely there was enough of that in the world.

Enos had never been false.

Kip pinched his thigh to stop the flood of thoughts that tried to break free. He felt Shadow's tail brush against his ankle.

"Perhaps."

As if to save him any embarrassment, Lord Blackmoor clapped his long hands together.

"I do believe dinner is ready. Shall we pass through?"

The dining room was a large oval, rich with wood-paneling, starting at the baseboards with polished oak, then turning to bookshelves a quarter of the way up the wall. They loomed over them, packed with their secrets.

The ceiling was an intricate window of stained-glass that took the shape of a coat of arms, the seal of Magic House; the manticores forever locked in battle. Moonlight streamed through the glass, illuminating each panel.

As irregular as it was, dinner waited for them on the table. Kip was sure he'd caught the hurried movements of a servant from behind a wall, fleeing the scene down some secret passageway.

Rather than traditional courses, the entire meal had been laid out at once. An entrée sat at each place setting, steam rising from seared meat and stewed vegetables. An intricate metal Plateau de Délices filled the center of the table, its curling metal rods each ending in a flat platter-shaped disk. Balanced on each of these was a bowl or plate filled with some new delight.

Green turtle soup.

Ballotines de Canard à la Cumberland.

Braised ox-tongue and spinach.

Seakale and butter sauce.

And the entrée of Boeuf braise à la Hussarde.

The dinner started in quiet awe as the guests helped themselves to the variety of dishes. Kip had never tasted anything so good. He wondered if magic had lent a hand in the kitchen. The hot dishes never seemed to lose their temperature, maintaining precisely the right warmth. The champagne stayed chilled in its flute, a slight frost etched on the glass.

Lord Blackmoor mostly watched his guests, a bemused smile on his face, occasionally catching Kip's eye as if there was some shared secret between them.

. . .

After an hour, Blackmoor rested his knife and fork on his plate, dabbed at his mouth, and addressed the group.

"You've all indulged an old man and listened to me prattle on, surely a wearying enterprise. For that, I thank you."

"Young in spirit, Francis!" Fairfield protested. "Young in spirit."

Blackmoor continued.

"But the point must be gotten to, and so the point I will get to."

He paused, Kip felt, for dramatic effect.

"There is a third wave coming, neither magic nor alchemy. You can feel the impatience, the fatigue, that surrounds our fine arts, as if there were more to discover, or more that we could offer.

"I believe Science is the cold evolution that approaches; the mere observation of the objective world, as if that could hold all the answers. This new discipline will dissect the world, but without any grace, without wonder."

Mr. Fairfield let out small clucking sound to note his displeasure.

"Now, Francis, certainly you don't believe such things? Every century has known its heretics. Why, Magic, the discipline that you most love, was the most maligned of all the arts. Would you burn us 'scientists' at the stake? The heretic become the norm over time. Perhaps we should shave our heads and repent."

With that Fairfield laughed and popped a grape into his mouth. Kip thought he could hear it crushed between his teeth.

"Is it a competition, Francis?" Britten asked. "Aren't we all striving towards the same goal? Why focus on the daily push and pull of the latest argument? I study the world that is just around the bend, just beyond our sight. You both do the same, after a manner."

Blackmoor scoffed. "Your work can't provide concrete answers. Spiritualism is a symptom of the new world; a return to nostalgia because of fear. It may comfort widows and widowers but what is its greater purpose? How much can we learn from a ghost, a shade, that haunts a world that's done with them?"

"Careful, Francis. Only old men fear the new." Fairfield said.

"I share my concern with you in particular, Stephen," Blackmoor said. "You once had a foot in both worlds, but, I fear, have jumped into the enemy's camp with your usual stubbornness."

"Yes, but how gingerly I jumped!"

The room tittered with light laughter. Kip looked down at Shadow who was now curled under his chair, either asleep or more interested in the view of everyone's feet.

"Your craft has its dangers, Francis," Fairfield continued. "Was it not a mere ten years ago that Dark House was finally shuttered, the twin to Magic House? We still have no accounting of what went on behind its walls. Why, its very form is now hidden from us, nothing but an empty lot adjacent to this residence. They say if you stare at the empty space at night, the stars bend, obscured by some shape that still resides there."

"Stuff and nonsense, surely," Lord Blackwell laughed. "Again the bias towards the magical arts. Dark House is gone, yes. You can look for the sinister, my good man, but you'll not find it."

Kip, too, had stared up at the empty space behind Magic House and thought he'd seen the very effect Fairfield mentioned. He'd even trained the Sulfur Glass on it once but with no result. It was simply an open lot now, protected by a rod-iron fence. The trees along its edges had moved closer, taking back the space with new growth.

"Don't damn the man because of his neighbor," Britten said. "Dark House is defunct and its mission still unknown, but to imply Lord Blackwell is somehow connected to it is... uncharitable. Stephen, would we judge you because of past actions of the Science Academy? I seem to remember the hybrid tests of 1872. Most unflattering."

Fairfield scoffed, taking a swig of wine. "The Science Academy is doing things unparalleled in history. Widening our gaze, we're looking out into the universe itself. Aren't there enough wonders in the physical world without all this faffing about? We've observed evidence of heavenly bodies of such immensity that light can't escape. They theorize that there are particles that can be in two places at once, or here and then across the universe in an instant. It challenges everything we know of our existence. Surely something so fascinating yet observable has more weight than ghosts and magic."

Britten pushed on. "You know my view, gentlemen. A spiritualist seeks no answers on this plane, but knows they're hidden from us, accessed only by the lucky few."

"Such as yourself?" Fairfield offered.

"Indeed. But I see no great difference between us. Do we not all seek the same goal? Truth?"

This caused another eruption, as everyone talked over one another, violently debating the point. Kip didn't see the purpose in such debates. He scanned the room, remaining silent, smiling politely when necessary, or laughing falsely so as not to be rude. His mind strayed back to his well at Alchemy House. He could almost see it, feel it; the hard cold stone, the damp chilled air.

"What does Master Kip think?" Blackmoor said, breaking Kip's daydream.

He could feel Shadow stir under the table.

"What do I think?" Kip asked, wondering what the answer was. "I think it's largely academic, isn't it?"

More tittering and dramatic gasps.

"I mean, surely it is," Kip continued. "There's objective *and* subjective truth, and there's shared subjective truth."

"Shared subjective truth?"

"Well, yes. Everything you see before us is a shared construct." Kip motioned to Lord Blackmoor. "You're only the master of Magic House because society has agreed that you are." He picked up his dessert spoon. "This spoon is laid horizontally above the plate because we've agreed that that's where cultured well-mannered people put it. London itself only runs because of a shared dream of reality. Laws, money, class, judgement, it all springs from a fever dream of reality."

Silence.

"I didn't realize Alchemists were nihilists as well."

Kip flushed. "Is it nihilism to say that we have made the world we live in, for better or worse? We've decided what's right, what's 'normal,' what power is...what love is."

The well again. It called to him, saying: *retreat from this and return to me. Put aside these petty debates and wasted hours. Humanity will wage these debates without you, forever.* He wanted to hear the drums again, those awful drums.

"Then what is your bird's eye view of it all?" Fairfield asked. "What does it all mean?"

Kip continued.

"I simply wonder if man's path is towards enlightenment, or the other way. The soul and spirit of man are bound to the body. The corporeal form is a blockage. If we're going to become what we were meant to be, we must be purified."

But the words that had once sounded so rich in his ears, felt shallow, rehearsed. Was he living by any of these principles? If anyone had been purified, it was Enos, his essence scattered by death.

Blackmoor spoke, "the alchemic concept that by destroying matter, you draw out its soul."

"Stuff and nonsense, respectfully," Fairfield snapped.

"Everything is moving towards perfection," Kip said. "Whether it's minerals in the ground, coal becoming a diamond, a body revealing its essence.

"Iteration and perfection, there's a crossover there. Iteration is the closest thing to perfection before its iterated upon once again. The target is always moving."

"Precocious youth, isn't he?" Britten said.

"Precocious indeed," Blackmoor said, not unkindly. "Master Kip, perhaps you could explain the overarching truth of your studies, the purpose?"

Kip hadn't come here to share, but he felt the sudden need to speak. All his tinkering in the shadows, all his waiting, all those grand ideas that no one got to hear. Blackmoor had given him the slightest nudge, but it was all he needed.

"Well, it's less academic and more an art form. There are three basic principles that define alchemy. They're not just chemical, but philosophical.

"Sulfur represents the soul, the life force that moves through our body.

"Mercury is the animating force, the spirit that binds our 'soul' to the physical world.

"Salt denotes the physical body, our biological form. It's the vessel that houses the spirit and soul.

"Together they make a unifying force, the Soul of All Things. Unlock these principles and you unlock the deepest secret there is, the power of life itself."

The power to bring back Enos.

Shadow rose up on his hind legs, his two paws on the table's edge, and peaked at the silent dinner table.

"Sulfur, mercury, and salt," Fairfield said. "There's a quaintness to it that appeals."

"I think it's far more noble than that," Blackmoor said. "If you'll forgive me, Master Kip, it's magic in the age of reason. Everything starts with magic, with the seed of an idea and the hope that it may bear fruit."

"Sulfur, mercury, and salt," Britten echoed wistfully.

"I think we need some refreshment, if we're to continue this debate," Blackmoor added.

He rang a silver bell on the table.

Kip was surprised to see no valet. Blackmoor's own daughter, Clover, entered the room instead, carrying a silver tray with a collection of small cordials on it. Again Kip felt himself shrink from her.

How her father could summon such an overwhelming string of words while his daughter had none was a great injustice. It was made worse by Mr. Blackmoor's profession, a career that depended on his voice, drawing forth magic with the spoken word. If she had the ability, it would never be known. It was painful to see her reduced to a servant. Perhaps Mr. Blackmoor meant well by giving her such a position, but perhaps not.

Kip averted his eyes, looking down at his plate. He'd spilled a coin-sized drop of jam on the tablecloth, a small red stain that immediately embarrassed him. He placed his hand over it.

Clover circled the table, placing a cordial by each guest.

"Thank you, my dear," Blackmoor said.

The other guests barely noticed her, but as she approached Kip he looked up, catching her eye. Again a swell of anxiety washed over him. Her eyes expressed the thoughts that her mouth could not, brimming with hidden secrets. Kip had his secrets too, and one conspirator could always spot another.

Clover set the small glass of liquid at his place, crystalline-red against the table cloth.

"Thank you," he whispered, but she retreated quickly without any recognition. Shadow watched her as she left the room, a pale ghost speeding away.

"Now we may be refreshed, gentlemen, and my dear lady," Mr. Blackmoor declared. "Let us consume and ingest; in Latin, let us *vorō*, let us be *vorax*. To our good health and continued pursuit of the capital–T–'Truth'!"

They raised their glasses and imbibed. The cordial was warm in the mouth, slightly viscous but so smooth that Kip wondered if he had even drank it. He looked down at the remaining liquid in his glass, a tawny copper that swirled in the bottom like a tiny whirlpool. Kip caught a trace of valerian root. It was nearly masked by the alcohol, but it was there. There was something else too, something that sent a spike of alarm through his system, but it was too late.

A dull buzz filled his ears and he looked up to see Fairfield and Britten looking around the room, apparently hearing the same noise. It grew louder, thrumming in his skull.

"And now for dessert," Blackmoor spoke through the haze of noise.

6

A paralysis crept into Kip's muscles, locking his arm in place on the table; his glass still raised. He felt a weight in his chest and was suddenly aware of his lungs, filling and emptying their oxygen, streaming out his life-force.

Amelia Britten forced out words, each one punctuated with her labored breath.

"What. Have. You. Done. Blackmoor?"

"Only what is necessary. You have just ingested distilled hemlock laced with valerian root, a tincture of my own design, and one aided by magic. One cannot rely on roots and twigs alone like some damnable herbalist."

Fairfield made a weak choking sound, and Blackmoor looked his way. Kip saw his eyes and the madness there, marveling that he hadn't noticed it before.

"Don't trouble yourself, Fairfield. The tincture alone won't kill you. Perhaps the practitioners at the Science Academy can help you."

There was a sharp growl from under the table, and Shadow sprang into action. His small form split, finding every shadow in the room. Each bit of darkness vibrated; the outline of books on the shelves, the edge of dishes on the table, the forked shadows of the candelabra; they all moved in unison.

"You're bad," Shadow's echo-voice hissed, as the darkness descended on Blackmoor, stretching towards him like groping tentacles.

"Tiresome creature," Blackmoor said. He reached under the table and Kip heard a sharp *click*.

Blinding light shot from the top of each bookshelf, turning everything white. It was like an overexposed picture, fading everything into a white void. Kip looked at his hand extended in front of him, now like a white glove. For a moment, he thought he could see through the flesh itself, the bones of his hand grotesquely holding his cordial.

Shadow cried out as he was forced to retreat, each part of him pushed back until almost no shadows remained. He crawled his way across the table, and found the dim shadow of the Plateau de Délices for refuge. He remained there, immobilized.

"Stop. You'll kill him." Kip wheezed, forcing the words past the creeping paralysis, not knowing if Shadow could be killed, not wanting to find out.

"I'm just ensuring some decorum here," Blackmoor laughed. "Lord, do you two make a racket. Such dramatics."

He looked up at the ceiling.

"Arc lights, my boy. Two carbon electrodes that ionize gas. Never let it be said that I reject modernism." He smirked at Fairfield. "Now that that's out of the way, I will tell you a tale.

"Right now there are three shades, each in your image, boarding a boat in Surrey, a boat that will be lost at sea. Your presence will be logged with the harbor master, observed by the dock crew, and remarked upon by the general roustabouts of the wharf.

"Why three such luminaries were together will remain unknown, but perhaps it's not too surprising. Mediocrity often finds its twin, or triplet, in this case."

Blackmoor spoke some mumbled words, his eyes closed, as if he were willing himself into a trance. The repeated mantra left his lips, almost visible as it carried across the table. A blue fibrous light unwound from his mouth. It wove through serving plates and dimmed candles, inching across the tablecloth, and then to each place-setting, before coiling around each guest.

Kip had always been able to find calm in the middle of panic. He could make his way to the eye of any storm, so long as he focused, retreating from the moment. This time was no different. He watched Lord Blackmoor with dead eyes, studying each small movement, waiting for a clue to reveal itself, a clue to his motives, and a way out of this trap.

Blackmoor stopped speaking, his eyes snapped open, his neck craned painfully forward. Two pinpricks of red light shone in his eyes, two sharp embers in a fire. He raised his hands then clapped them together forcefully. The sound was dull and alien, not the sound of two hands meeting.

Blackmoor reached for a knife on the table, then brought it to his head. He cut off a lock of his silver-white hair and, with another mumbled incantation, offered it to the blue light that bobbed over the table.

It swallowed the offering with an intense greed, and then

snapped to life. Strands of black jumped from its center and spanned the room, like the net of a spiderweb.

Small pinpoints of light winked to life as the black threads thickened, until the full design came into view.

The stars, Kip thought. *He's opened a pathway to the stars.*

The star-scape enveloped the room making a dome above them, leaving only the table and the floor below. A bitter chill followed the vision as a new atmosphere seeped into the room. Kip saw his breath flow out in an icy cloud.

The star-scape expanded, revealing far-off galaxies spiraling through the blackness.

Blackmoor spoke, continuing the dinner party as if nothing had happened.

"Compromise and agreement are for the weak. That's the work of doubters and the cowards of Parliament, for the weak-willed agnostics who dither when they should commit. Magic is the truth of this world, hard-fought and future-proof. When you've unlocked the *Primum Dominum*, the Prime Mastery, you don't look elsewhere for data and opinion."

Kip looked down at the cordial still raised half way to his mouth. Frost had begun to form on the glass, its snowflake pattern moving towards his hand.

Francis Blackmoor was transformed, or perhaps revealed. He trained his red eyes on each of them.

"Spiritualism, the bastard cousin to magic."

He turned to Amelia Britten.

"I cast you out."

A *snap* in the air behind her, a sharp *crack* like breaking stone. Threads of the star-net sprung towards her like fine silk string, weaving around her body. They encircled her, binding her arms and legs, criss-crossing her chest and then pouring into her gaping mouth. She was nearly mummified when they jerked backwards, yanking her and her chair into the void behind her. The motion upset the table, spilling her drink and sending her plate to the floor where it shattered, its sound oddly dulled.

She gave a scream, a final shriek that didn't come from her mouth, but seemed to be psychically transmitted. It was a horrific sound that rang in Kip's ears long after it had stopped.

"Science, the small death by rationality."

Blackmoor turned to Stephen Fairfield.

"I cast you out."

Fairfield's eyes darted back and forth with a sickening panic, terror widening them. The same coils that had grabbed Britten, snaked around him and yanked him into the starry void.

Kip had seen powerful spells before, he'd seen Blackmoor himself perform them, but never anything like this. He felt his hair and clothing rise as if gravity no longer existed in the room. He strained to see Shadow out of the corner of his eye, but his friend was hidden from view, nearly absorbed by the arc lights.

Fairfield struggled in his chair as he floated in front of a backdrop of stars. He strained against the silken threads, his eyes rolling wildly.

His motion slowed to a slight twitching and then stopped completely. He joined Britten, the pair floating in a lazy ballet.

"Well, now that that unpleasantness is out of the way."

Blackmoor waved his hand and Kip felt the life flood back into his body. The chill of the stars vanished immediately, replaced with an artificial warmth. The room was just a dining room again, now absent two guests.

Released from the effects of the potion, Kip grabbed a knife and pushed back his chair, knocking it to the floor. He retreated to the back of the room, his back against one of the bookshelves.

He waited for the tide of fear to roll in, wishing it would wash over him. But, even now, it didn't come. Kip brandished the knife, gleaming like white hot steel under the arc lights.

"Please turn them off."

Mr. Blackmoor smiled. "Will your creature behave?"

"Yes."

"And will you? You think to stab me with that knife, to kill me with something so quaint?"

"If I must."

"And why wouldn't I cast you into the void with our late and unfortunate guests? Where do you think they are now? Floating in the firmament? Mingling in Saturn's rings? Saturn's in retrograde, I hear. It must be peaceful to float out there, a relief to no longer carry the burdens of the world, just light and shadow in the vacuum of the cosmos."

Blackmoor smiled. "The cold, Kip. Did you feel it? I thought it would be enough to get a rise out of even you."

"Turn off the lights!"

Another click threw the room into darkness.

"To me, Shadow," Kip whispered harshly. He heard his friend whimper, then felt the creature reform behind him, the strands of his body weaving back together. His paw-like fingers tugged anxiously at Kip's leg.

The candles on the table reignited. Blackmoor smiled, a glint of teeth in the half-light, then raised his glass.

"Please sit, Master Kip."

"I'll stand, thank you."

"Very well."

The magician sat back in his chair.

"There are two roads, Kip. One is the free sharing of ideas and the challenging of conventions, as the so-called great minds of our time argue over the nature of our world. The endless debates and impassioned voices that say 'consider me' and 'validate me,' no matter how asinine their viewpoint.

"The second road, now that's a more twisted path. It's narrow enough that one must walk it alone, but that lonely pilgrimage, that's the only route to true knowledge. It is hard-won but pure and true.

"And when you've walked that road your disgust for those who haven't grows. How dare lesser minds question the pilgrim when he holds the capital—T—Truth at his breast. How dare the wisdom of Magic House be questioned as we barrel towards a new century. Are we to enter it in a weakened state of uncertainty? Or close our hand into a fist and strike?

"Magic has served the world since the dawn of time. It is all that we need, and all that I will allow.

"Meanwhile, you're chasing logic with your elements and atoms, trying to find order. Alchemists believe that every element has undeveloped potential, do they not? That the imperfect can be made perfect. And this is why you spend your time, back bent and fingers stained, to find some perfection in the world? Surely you know there's no such thing?"

"Not perfection. Purity," Kip said.

"I see no difference."

"You, for example, have no purity, you're stained by power and now murder."

Blackmoor tutted softly.

"You want the world to match your wild imaginings. You want to prove your intuitions instead of create something new from them. You're like our recently departed scientist. You try to turn your fanciful ideas into facts."

"And why are you better?"

"Because I don't bother with all that. Magic is fantasy made manifest. I don't give a toss for observation and proof-gathering. The truth is what I say it is. Before tonight would you have believed the truth that a man could open a portal to the stars and cast his enemies through it?"

Kip felt the balance of the knife in his hand. The metal felt cold, too cold. Shadow still pawed at his leg, digging his claws into his flesh.

"And why have you spared me? It would seem Alchemy House is no friend to you."

"For precisely one reason, the secret in your basement."

Kip shrank back and, for the first time, felt the small icy prick of fear. It worked between his ribs, slipping into his heart.

"I...I don't know what you mean."

Lord Blackmoor laughed, but there was no humor in his voice. It was a dead sound that echoed across the room. His laugh stopped as suddenly as it had started, his jaw snapping shut like a snake's.

"Lie to me again, and I kill you."

Kip knew that he meant it. He was tangling with a madman now.

Blackmoor knitted his hands together until his knuckles turned white. He leaned forward.

"There is one thing that the Alchemists hold dear, one idea that they cling to: that the mystery of death can be revealed. You wish to find the Primal Element, The Soul of all Things, to aid that purpose. You have done something in that basement, something you should have not.

"And if you believe that I will let some child, some fucking homosexual, uncover the greatest mystery the world has ever known, then you are mistaken."

A small sound escaped Kip's lips, some part of him trying to escape. He couldn't stand how transparent he was, how obvious his desires were. He was a pariah, laughed at behind closed doors. *Just some fucking homosexual with his obsessions.*

Unrelenting, Blackmoor continued. "You will tell me what you've done in Alchemy House, tell me its purpose, and tell me how I may control it. I will go and see this wonder for myself and I will claim it. Then I will burn Alchemy House to the ground."

Kip lowered the knife to his side. Lord Blackmoor had done his work. His secrets seemed so selfish now, once dragged into the light. The endless cycle of pining and self-pity that had nourished him for so long. The addiction to his own thoughts, recalling again and again every hurt, every wound. And the one face hovering above it all; Enos, with his green eyes and raven hair.

And his smile.

And his voice.

And his scent.

"I can't tell you something I know nothing about," Kip said. His voice was steady but he felt the sting of tears in his eyes.

Blackmoor was quick to notice. "Your tears say enough. Enough, at least, to reveal your secrets. How did you do it?"

"I...I didn't do anything. I just wished for it to be."

But 'wished' wasn't the right word. There was no word for what he'd done.

Blackmoor was leaning forward now, a look of expectation on his face. *More like hunger*, Kip thought.

"I wished to see someone dear to me," Kip continued, "someone beyond my reach." Even now he couldn't say it. *Someone dead*. "And that wishing brought forth...a portal."

Blackmoor's smile was grotesque. "The most ancient question of all, the question that's founded religions, caused civilizations to rise and crumble, and you did it for some poxy lover, some fellow bender to share in your abominations."

Kip dropped the knife to the floor. He felt the cold again, not sure if it was in his mind or not. Whatever fight had been in him was gone. He looked down at Shadow, still scared and vulnerable.

"As an Alchemist, you should know better than anyone, the elements of the flesh are the weakest of all.

"Very well, if you brought this portal into existence, then you will remain alive while I learn its secrets."

Lord Blackmoor rang the silver bell on his table once again, summoning his daughter back into the room. Again she came like a wraith, her eyes as empty as before. She took her place at her father's side but there was no connection between them. She might have been just another object in the house. Her white hair hung in her face, masking any expression.

Blackmoor's eyes never left Kip.

"Step forward," he said.

Kip and Shadow stepped forward two paces, looking down at the floorboards.

Again Blackmoor flipped the switch at his side, charging the arc lights. They burst to life.

A ripple of energy charged through the air around them as Blackmoor muttered an incantation once again; again the glint of embers in his eyes, red coal buried in the black.

A rending *crack* sounded beneath Kip's feet and he watched as the floorboards began to heave and buckle, then fall away. Stars peaked out between the falling boards, and the chill of the darkness rose up to meet him. The table and chairs followed the floor, spiraling into the star-scape below. He watched as his unfinished cordial spilled and tumbled downwards, the liquid exploding into droplets before freezing into perfect spheres.

He saw his bag resting on a bookshelf across the room. If only he could get to it.

The only bits of floor that remained were the broken, toothy pieces that Kip and Shadow balanced on, like two nests suspended in air. Shadow was nearly faded to nothing now. He whined and clawed weakly at the floor, flinching from the beams of the arc lights.

"The floor you're standing on will continue to shrink, completely disappearing after one hour. A small assurance that, if I were to not return, you would follow me to the grave."

"You're a little man," Kip said.

Bright beams spilled into the void, making thick streams of light.

"Sometimes it takes little men to do great things. The world is a contradiction, Master Kip."

He gestured to the fallen world below.

"Does your alchemy allow for such things, Master Kip?

You've played with things that you should have left alone. Let's see if I can make use of them."

Blackmoor turned, deliberately showing Kip his back as if to make a final wall between them.

"Come, daughter," he said. "We have much to do."

The pair turned and left the room. Only the cold remained.

7

Reveal your secrets, Lord Blackmoor thought, running his hand over the wooden door of Alchemy House, then finding the handle that looked like blue metal in the moonlight.

A simple unlocking spell and he could feel the heavy bolts slide out of place. *How wonderful it is when the world gives itself over to you*, he thought, as he stepped inside.

He could smell the scent of an extinguished fire as he groped forward, trying to find some anchor in the darkness.

The house is asleep, he thought. *It has slept for too long, occupied by a child and his beast.*

The three houses should have come to him, were there any justice in the world. Magic House reigned supreme, but Alchemy House and Dark House were the other legs of the stool. Symmetry and balance were all that he asked for. Discipline. Not the loose freedoms of the modern age. He remembered a time when a master had ruled each house and had worked together for the good of the Empire.

Something damp brushed against his face and he

cringed, bringing his arms up. He reached out slowly, feeling the object, then tracing its shape with his fingertips. It was a leaf. He felt its thick and waxy form, then the branch it was attached to.

He felt displaced, wondering why a tree would be growing here, wondering what its purpose might be.

Where is my mind? he thought suddenly, then reached into his pocket. He pulled out a small vial and felt for the cork. The tiny *popping* sound it made when removed sounded like a snap-cracker going off. He tilted the vial, and the dust inside, onto his fingers, then rubbed them together. Small blue sparks jumped from his fingertips and became a steady flame that rested just above his palm. Light flooded the house. The shadow of the tree branches projected into the room.

I'm lost in a forest.

The light would be his guide. Magic would seek out magic.

The light in his palm tugged him gently, leading him through the house. He was in a room with a stone hearth, the black hole of the fireplace a yawning mouth, waiting to be fed. Above the mantel hung a portrait, all blue and black in the shadows.

Was this Kip's obsession? Another youth to practice his perversions on. The immorality of youth was no surprise to him. His own daughter had once been a disobedient and willful child.

Through the fireplace, is that where I'm meant to go? That had a certain poetry to it; passing through fire to gain knowledge. He stepped into the hearth and pushed at its back wall. It gave under the pressure, a chasm opening into deeper blackness.

He moved down a chilled tunnel that ended in a wooden

staircase. As he descended, he saw it, finally getting an answer to a long-asked question.

Everything that has eluded me is made clear. Even as he thought that, he couldn't be sure why. It was a hole in the ground, filled with blackness. *Why does it hold such power?*

Blackmoor approached its edge, his footsteps quiet on the earthen floor. Craning his neck, he stared into the abyss. It was in that moment that his certainty left him. A small clawing thought entered his mind: was he prey that had come willingly to the predator? His stomach churned as the blackness below mesmerized him.

"What...what are your secrets?" he whispered.

Silence.

Then an echo, as if his own voice were speaking back.

"There are no secrets between us. You've told me everything. You've spilled your heart's blood into this well, with each thought, each wish, each desire. I know you like the course of my veins as they pump my lifeblood."

It's not talking to me, is it? It thinks I'm Kip. Blackmoor felt a rising panic. It would be best to declare himself, declare his ownership.

"I am Lord Francis Blackmoor of Magic House and I demand to know the nature of this well."

Silence again.

A cold breeze shot up through the circle of stone. The voice turned to ice.

"You're new. Come closer."

Blackmoor obeyed without hesitation, craning his neck further over the well. The blackness gave way to a faint light, a sickly green glow, like small bioluminescent creatures moving in a tidal pool. The movement made him dizzy.

"I have come...to learn secrets," Blackmoor said, finding

it hard to form the words.

"Yours or mine?" the darkness asked. "Mine are terrible and wonderful and not for this world. Where is the boy?"

Blackmoor's mouth was dry now, so dry that he could barely speak.

"I took him," he rasped. "I imprisoned him. There were reasons." He found himself reciting the monologue he'd shared with Kip, the summation of his ideas. It came out like a poorly read script. "There are two roads. One is the free sharing of ideas and the challenging of conventions—"

"Silence," the blackness said calmly.

There was silence. The sounds of Alchemy House filled the void; the soft creaking of wood as a house continually settles, and an odd breathy sigh as if he could hear every inhale and exhale.

Blackmoor imagined the branches and leaves moving in time to the sound.

"You're so different, different than the boy. Are all of you so different? The boy is pure and beautiful, even with his sadness. He wears it well.

"But you, you're pointy and dangerous, aren't you? You're all wants and anger and righteousness. That's boring. Does it bother you that you're boring?"

Blackmoor's fingers tightened against the stone, forming two claws. He thought he would shatter the well, shatter the house, with his tension.

"There are so many down here like you. They had ideas too. They thought their beliefs would save them. Do you think the plasma of a star cares about your beliefs? Or the particles that skip across the universe, blinking in and out of existence?

"You can do your little magic tricks and think you're a

great man, a mover of history, but you're no different than the villains who have come before you."

Blackmoor wanted to protest, but found it difficult to speak. *I'm the hero not the villain*, he thought. *Doesn't this thing know that?*

"This very night you've taken lives because of your beliefs. I can see the aura of death around you. Death is a disruption. Did you think it wouldn't leave a mark?"

Blackmoor's eyes grew wide. He wanted to blink but couldn't pull them away from the hypnotic green light.

"How...how did you come to be?" he struggled to ask.

"The boy wished it."

This doesn't make sense, Blackmoor thought. *He wished it? There is no power of magic or alchemy to wishes. They are the limp fantasies of a child.*

"Wishes...are the stuff of children," he said to the black pit.

"Are they? If you say so. Yet here you are, wishing just as the boy did. You're practically on your knees. In fact, let's see you there..."

And it was done. Blackmoor's legs weakened and shook, before collapsing. He fell to his knees in the dirt, a small cloud of dust circling him. His fingers still clamped the stone and his eyes stayed locked to the blackness below, his chin nearly rested on the rim of the well.

"It's a wishing well," Blackmoor whispered. The thought triggered something in him and he didn't know if he wanted to laugh or scream. It was all so absurd, all so counter to his vast knowledge. It defied everything.

Then he heard the sound of drums and the slithering of branches behind him. Vines and leaves coiled around his arms, holding them in place. He wanted to run; Lord Blackmoor had never wanted anything so badly. He would have given up everything in that moment, sped screaming from London, content to live a quiet life in some insipid countryside. But he also wanted to stare down into the well. Perhaps it's all he'd ever wanted. There was a black heart down there, blacker than his own, and it drew him closer.

He'd heard whispers from Dr. Fairfield, before his recent demise, that heavenly bodies moved in the cosmos, things of immensity and blackness that drew all other things to them. He had found his own immensity now.

"What do you wish for, Lord Blackmoor of Dark House?"

Blackmoor's eyes grew wider.

"How do you know I wish for anything? No one knows."

"It's written on your heart, plain to see."

"I only wished for the pursuit of truth, that's all I've ever wanted. All I want still. I want to find Dark House again so that I may share its secrets."

"There are shapes to the universe that you can't comprehend, edges that defy reason, that bend truth."

"Parliament had no right to attack a pillar of discovery, to defunct an entire school of thought."

Dark House had left on its own, following its own timeline. But Blackmoor was convinced it had known they were coming for it. It had *known*.

"You're a tiresome thing, an ant moving a grain of sugar. And yet, there is something we can do for each other. You want to know the secrets of death, and I want to know the secrets of life."

Blackmoor didn't want to know anything anymore. He just wanted quiet, to be nestled safely somewhere, but it was too late. The void had a form.

"What does it feel like to be alive?"

8

The dining room was a shadow now, almost lost to the weight of the stars.

Blackmoor hadn't returned. What had he found in Kip's basement, or what had found him? Kip thought he knew, but couldn't bring himself to ponder it; Lord Blackmoor poring over his secrets, exposing parts of him that should have remained hidden.

The floorboards had almost entirely dissolved at their feet. The star-scape rotated on an unseen axis and Kip had to close his eyes or be taken over by it. More furniture had fallen away. All the room's finery was being stripped and sent into the void.

Shadow was at his side, his form still paled by the arc lights. Their bodies burned like two candles, every inch of them illuminated in a sea of black. His friend mewled weakly, somehow injured by the light. Kip didn't know the limits of Shadow's powers, or his vulnerabilities.

He lowered his arms, his hands no longer shielding his eyes, and felt the silver bracelet slide down his wrist. The twin to Enos's bracelet. Even now, with death imminent, he couldn't escape the thought of him. It turned like a key pushing past tumblers, unlocking a door.

Then his mind barked a thought back.

Magnetism.

Even now the bracelets were attracted to one another. It was his own alchemy. He remembered the force of it, strong enough to tug at his arm, and pull him towards Enos, wherever he might be in the world. If it had worked before, it would work now.

Kip turned the small dial on the rim of the bracelet, touching the two metals, and felt them activate, a subtle buzz of energy that he had been trained to observe.

He could *feel* the other bracelet, tucked into the pocket of his bag on the bookshelf across the room. It was just beyond the wall of stars and in danger of fading out forever.

Kip thrust his hand out and felt a shudder of motion. The green bag tipped towards him, one handle tugging in his direction.

I have to get closer, just the slightest bit closer, he thought, then looked down at the patch of floorboards he stood on. They continued shrinking down to nothing.

He inched forward on creaking wood, its edges dissolving by the second, and leaned his body out over the void, nothing to support him.

He extended his hand again.

The bag slid a foot towards him on the bookshelf, toppling a small ivory statue that fell into the star-scape below, a spinning white blaze.

Closer.

"Shadow," Kip said as calmly as he could.

The creature stirred, his blue eyes now two slits as he

tried to block out the light. Even now, he tried to help, raising himself up on weakened arms.

"I need to get closer to my bag, Shadow! Just the smallest bit would do it. The bracelets weren't meant to be powerful. They were just a toy, a compass to nudge me in the right direction. But I think they're just powerful enough."

Shadow nodded and uncurled his body. The light cut through him, burning transparent swathes out of his form. His platform of floorboards had floated above Kip's. Shadow crawled to the edge and peered down. He would have to jump.

Jump down and over the abyss below.

Shadow's small fingers gripped the edge of the wood and he opened his eyes as wide as he could, the blue swirling with pain. His body coiled like a cat and then he pounced.

The movement was graceful at first until his hind leg caught the lip of his platform and he began to spin. His body nearly disappeared as it filled with starlight. Kip scrambled to catch him, hoping Shadow would even be visible by the time he got there.

The moment drew out, freezing time. He thought he could hear the ticking of the grandfather clock in the corner, counting every second with its heavy weight.

Kip extended his arms, unsure now if anything was above him.

I just had my friend commit suicide, he thought.

Then the weight hit him, a roiling mass of shadow in his arms. Kip locked his forearms around it, and dropped to his knees to keep his balance. Shadow's face appeared from the dark mass, a slight smile there.

"Let's go home," his friend whispered.

"Yes, let's!"

Kip looked to the bookshelf and his bag, now teetering over the edge.

"I need an anchor. Can you wrap your tail around the bottom of the platform?"

Shadow nodded and got into place. Kip took his hand.

"Ready?"

Kip leaned over the edge, flying over stars. He felt their coldness closing in just as it had on Britten and Fairfield.

If the bag falls, we're ruined.

Kip shot his arm out again, willing every muscle to stretch. His fingers clawed outward. He felt Shadow's body expanding, tipping him further over the void.

The bag shuddered, began to slide over the edge of the bookshelf, and then rocketed forward, all kinetic energy. It spun in a straight line directly to Kip. He grabbed the handles as it pushed him back with its force. Shadow supported him, before the two collapsed onto the wood.

A thin layer of frost covered the bag. Kip cracked it open, his mind racing.

Restoration, he thought; the process of restoring an element to its original form. If he could recall the elements that made up the dining room, stitching them together one by one, they'd be saved.

Kip took out a glass jar sealed with wax and ripped off the covering in thick shreds. The shimmering liquid sloshed in the jar and he steadied it with both hands to prevent it from spilling.

The dissolving platform disappeared under Kip's shoe, no more than three feet around.

He rooted through a leather pouch and found the starter agent, a small dried ball, no bigger than a rifle shot. This one contained the elements of wood; carbon, oxygen, and a few binding elements. He dropped it into the liquid and it began to smoke and bubble. Kip let out a hiss as it poured over the top and stung his hands, but he didn't dare let go. Instead, he scooped his cupped fingers into it and threw the liquid in a straight line from their platform to the door.

At first the fluid fell uselessly into the abyss, tiny drops of shimmering liquid speeding towards the stars.

Kip wanted to scream, but there was no time. He wanted to do so much, but there was no time.

Instead, he continued spooning out the liquid, coating the edge of their piece of floorboard and watching as the axis of the stars rotated again.

You'll never escape our gravity, they seemed to say.

Then something began to hiss and smoke. Thin brown veins appeared where the floor had been, moving outward in straight lines; some stick-straight, others wavering. They were tracing the pattern of the wood, bringing it back to life. Kip thought of the rings in a tree and his nervous mind wanted to count them all, each new one a better chance of them living. They continued to grow as the floor was restored around them. The veins traced the pattern of the floor and then turned at a right angle, finding the wall and bookshelves.

Kip swept his arm in a wide arc, sending the remaining liquid flying. Like paint strokes, each one filled in the form of the dining room until the world had returned to normal. The star-scape was contained by wood and books, a hearth and the stained-glass ceiling above.

There were non-reactive spots that his restoration liquid didn't seem to effect, small holes in reality where the stars still peeked through. Kip looked down at his feet, their platform of wood now no different than the rest of the floor. He took one hesitant step forward, testing the reformed surface. It would hold.

He ran forward and grabbed a small metal box from the bookshelf. He weighed it in his hand and then threw it at the row of arc lights. The first one shattered in an explosion of sparks, and triggered a chain-reaction, destroying each in turn. The blazing light was cut off as hot pinpricks filled the room; stars replaced with burning embers.

The blaze of the arc lights still danced in Kip's eyes as they stumbled into the street, throbbing circles of white. More than the arc lights was the memory of the star-scape, the way it yawned open, calling for them. Worlds had unfolded before them. They'd seen farther than any telescope.

Too far.

"The stars. Did Kip see all the stars?" Shadow asked.

"I saw them, Shadow."

Kip turned his head, straining to see the empty lot behind Magic House. It was focused darkness. He squinted, trying to find any trace of Dark House. Was it still there? Lord Blackmoor had gone mad, surely the only explanation. Had the madness come from somewhere close by? A star glinted in the sky; a barely visible wink, before returning to normal.

Kip ran a comforting hand down his friend's back, his body rippling under his palm.

"Lord Blackmoor knows, somehow he knows what I've done. We have to hurry back to Alchemy House. Are you up for it, my friend?"

In answer, Shadow raised his body up, standing on his

hind legs, and smiled. His form melted into a dozen pieces, bouncing from shadow to shadow in the street. Kip could see a ripple of him moving up a lamppost, then across a windowsill; moving between cobblestones like dark rainwater, before snapping back together.

"Shadow wants to gnaw on Lord Blackmoor's face," he said proudly.

"So do I."

The two ran side-by-side through abandoned streets, weaving their pattern through a sleeping London. Kip thought he could hear echoes of the drumbeat from his well, finding him even here. It was like a voice calling to him, but when he turned his head the sound vanished.

Kip thought of Fairfield and Britten, cast into the stars, their shades on a doomed vessel in the Atlantic. He imagined his own shade drowning in that shipwreck somewhere off the coast of England. Water rushing in, sinking tarred-timber and canvas sails, as they swirled to the bottom of the sea. What happened to a drowned shade? Did it vanish or remain, untouched and lifeless, in the depths? Some future ocean explorer would find a preserved boy sleeping through the decades on a bed of seaweed.

The drumbeat strengthened as they approached Aldgate Street. He felt the gnawing bite of anxiety as his secret spilled out into London, for all to see. The secret that he'd formed without skill or discipline, making it all the more shameful.

The tower of Alchemy House loomed in the distance, a black cut in a blacker sky.

Kip reached into his bag and pulled out the Sulfur Glass. It was already vibrating, like a crystal overloaded with sound. He looked through it, at the place that had been his home for so long, and saw a structure under assault. Black ribbons swirled around it like searching fingers, anchoring to cobblestones and railings.

The ashen branches had matured. No longer saplings, they had exploded with the force of springtime, breaking through windows and wrapping themselves around the tower. Thin blue light was woven into the branches, moving in constant flux, sometimes sparking into a deep and violent purple.

A figure approached, only a silhouette in the Sulfur Glass. Kip dropped the glass plate to his side.

"Hey, Magic Boy," said the thing that had been Ragman. His skin was as gray as the tree limbs and looked like ancient paper wrapped over bone, pulled tight as a drum. His overcoat hung in shreds, the ribbons of fabric now turned black and moving around him, pulled by an invisible force.

Kip scanned the ground and saw the perimeter of the darkness. It was still limited by something, spilling into their world but not strong enough to escape the pull of Alchemy House and the well. There was still time.

"Your secrets, boy," Ragman said, gesturing behind him. "All your toiling and waiting, your crying and longing; it bore fruit, black fruit."

"You're not yourself, Ragman," Kip said.

"To be sure, boy. To be sure. My hunger is gone, for food at least. My need for the bottle has vanished like a breaking fever.

"An apparition came to me and whispered in my ear. Oh, the things it told me. It said it came from a dark place, but had finally seen the light. It said the master of the house was a golden boy, all the riches of alchemy wrapped in his flesh."

"I have to get to my house, Ragman."

Ragman sneered. He barred his rotten teeth. Kip thought the expression would tear his face in two.

"Maybe the gold is buried in your heart. Let's rip it out and see."

The beggar's shape began to change. Muscle and bone turned to wood as his arms ripped through his clothes. His fingers fused into coiled vines as smaller branches sprouted from his body.

Shadow growled. Kip's hand slipped into the pouch he kept in his pocket. He dusted it with the filament powder and then extended it towards the approaching beggar. It sparkled under the moonlight, a thousand grains of dust at his command.

Kip snapped his fingers together and ignited the powder. It sprang to life with a violent burst, showering Ragman's face with light, showing every vein and wrinkle and glinting off his teeth.

The flame wove around Ragman's face and lit the hair on his head like kindling. His battered top hat went up next, the flames rising like a candle.

A sound burst from Ragman that could have been a scream or a laugh, a hysterical bit of madness. It ran on and on. He flailed, trying to beat down the flames on his head, but only managed to light his tree-limb arms. Blue flame spread up the branches as they seethed in anger.

Kip turned and fled, Shadow at his side. They ran towards the house, the screams of Ragman in their ears.

Don't look back, Kip thought.

Alchemy House was expanding and contracting, awakened by the disturbance. The tree limbs moved like roiling snakes, tightening their grip. Kip heard the wood creaking under the pressure and the high-pitched shattering of glass.

The tower above them swayed against the stars, now fully absorbed by the forest around it.

The front door loomed ahead, wreathed in leaves. Kip extended his flaming palm, the blue light jumping from finger to finger. Its coolness had already given way to warmth and he wondered how long before it would start to burn.

The limbs recoiled, shivering and moving away from the door, leaving tracks of stripped paint behind. The door swung open, a dark cavern behind it. They heard Ragman roar. Kip turned to see him in full rage, his tree-limb arms grown longer, forming new branches, some with budding black flowers. He ran towards the house.

Kip crossed the doorframe, but could have crossed into a different world. The thick air seemed to carry no sound but dull echoes.

And drums.

Small filaments filled the air. They were illuminated by the fire in Kip's palm, now a burning itch. He knew Ragman was close behind but time seemed to have slowed. Each step was deliberate, every movement planned, even the beating of his heart.

The foyer was a bird's nest of tangled branches. Kip and Shadow wove through the maze, ducking here and climbing there, clawing their way towards the parlor and the hearth. The outstretched branches pulled at them, grabbing clothing and scraping flesh. A shadow cut off the light behind them.

"Your golden heart, boy." The words slurred and warped. "It belongs to me."

Ragman came on, pulling at the snarl of branches, his hair and hat still smoking. He looked like he was swimming towards them.

Kip made it to the hearth and fell to his knees, the fire in his palm now burning sharply. He passed it onto the dry logs in the fireplace and watched as they came to life. The tree limbs shuddered as the fire crackled. He could hear a nervous inhalation of breath throughout the house.

Shadow looked back anxiously. "Shadow can fight him. Shadow can bite him."

"No!" Kip snapped. "Transmutation, that's the answer, the joining of one thing to another."

Part congelation and part digestion.

Ragman howled, pushing and tearing and breaking. Some of the branches moved out of the way, and those that didn't were reduced to splinters.

Shadow flattened himself against the wall.

"Is there time for Kip's experiments?"

Kip didn't answer but slipped his bag from his back. He dug through the ancient collection of vials and powders, searching for the proper ingredients. One by one, he added elements to the fire; a brown glass bottle emptied its contents, two pinches from a leather pouch, a thin liquid that moved like mercury. The fire took the ingredients greedily, sparking as it transformed them.

It would be crude, but hopefully effective.

"What is separated can be joined."

Kip cupped his hands and brought them into the fire. The heat stayed back, but it was there, inching closer and closer. He scooped up a handful of the fire and turned to face Ragman.

His shadow filled their world as he reared up, demon eyes blazing. His branch-arms twisted into knots and rough wood. Bark spread to his face, carving out wooden features.

"Fool's gold," he sneered as he reached towards Kip.

Kip brought up his hands, the delicate flame moving there, and blew into his palms. The flame exploded into a blizzard of sparks. Kip's face turned scarlet from the flash. Shadow melted farther into the wall, his body cut by the light.

It spread outward like flaming dust and sped towards Ragman. The particles covered his body, boring into wood and flesh, tiny blue and purple daggers of light. He screamed.

The branches in the parlor retracted as he tripped backwards, trying to escape, his limbs flailing. But it was too late. The Transmutation powder created some magnetism, drawing wood to wood. Green shoots sprang from the branches and found each other, tying themselves into knots. The new growth bound Ragman's arms, slowly lifting him off the ground as he fused with the trees around him.

Kip saw the terrible strain on Ragman's body, and realized he wasn't just being held in place, but pulled in all directions. He heard the sharp *pop* of cracking wood, then looked away.

"I'm sorry, Ragman. I'm so sorry."

Kip jumped through the fire in the hearth, pushing open the stone door to the basement, and hurried down the corridor. After a few paces he turned back.

"Don't look, Shadow!" he called.

But his friend stood in the doorway of the fireplace. If Kip squinted he could see Shadow's blue eyes shining through the back of his head. The creature stood stone-still and watched as a horrible scream filled the air. More wood splintering and then a final guttural sound.

The echo of the scream had barely faded when it was replaced by another, this one further down the tunnel. Kip spun around and hurried to the top of the wooden staircase. Shadow pattered along and joined him, resting his paws on the railing.

A silhouette hung in the air above the well, pitch-black except for a tuft of white hair. Lord Blackmoor's arms hung at his side, his head lolled against his chest. He looked like a marionette put away for the night, suspended by his strings. A black haze moved around him, flowing clockwise around the room. The branches moved like snakes, but seemed hesitant to touch him.

Kip held up the Sulfur Glass.

The world he viewed through it was an explosion of color, violent in its hue. Slashes of red light cut into the stone, claw marks covered the floor.

The glass in his hand vibrated as the snaking lines of light coiled together. It looked like the splattering of luminescent blood, lighting a crime scene. The glass was a small earthquake now, shaking the image in its frame.

With a violent *crack*, it shattered. The slivers of glass caught the red light as it fractured and fell to the floor. Only a small piece remained, clutched in Kip's hand. Without thinking, he put it in his pocket, then looked back to the well.

The haze pulsed, solidifying as a voice rose from it. It spoke in an alien tongue that sounded like speech running backwards. The ribbons of black drew into Lord Blackmoor. They found his eyes and mouth, searched out his nostrils, and flowed into his body. He twitched as they invaded him. The voice faded with the vapor, turning to a whisper.

The thing that had been Lord Blackmoor opened its eyes, two blue circles, and then lifted its head. There was a smile on its face, white teeth gleaming in a black frame.

"This is what it feels like," it said.

Then it fell. The marionette's strings were cut and it plummeted into the well, gone in a blur.

The moment the thing vanished, the circling boughs turned on Kip and Shadow. They formed bars of wood, blocking off the entrance back to the hearth. Some turned to searching tentacles, sniffing out their prey. Kip jumped down to the dirt floor, hoping to use the wooden staircase as a shelter, but they found him there, breaking through wood, then lifting the staircase from the ground with a grinding *screech*.

The beams of wood slid from the ground like pulled teeth, leaving gaping holes behind. Limbs wove around what remained of the structure then pulled it upward with a tremendous force, splintering it to pieces against the ceiling. Chips of wood rained down on them along with a fine cloud of sawdust.

Kip almost didn't notice. He was filled with a covetous madness, watching the voice in the well take Blackmoor; his enemy going before him into a world that he'd brought forth. All sense left him, all the anxious restraint he'd shown for the last year, the feeble waiting. Whatever lay beneath that stone was his to explore, not Blackmoor's.

Shadow split his form and ran into the writhing nest of branches as they wove across the floor. He gnawed at the bark, tore at the leaves, but it had no effect.

Kip backed up against the well, feeling the cold and familiar stone on his back. But its tranquilizing effect was gone. Now it was only a threat.

It was always a threat.

He reached into his bag and the maroon pouch within and grabbed a handful of the fixation dust. He knew fire was the only thing that would keep back wood. He struggled to light the powdered dust on his hand, small sparks falling to the floor.

Shadow returned to his side, breathing heavily.

"Shadow can't cut down trees," he panted.

The branches sped towards them now, all hunters closing for a kill. Kip's palm ignited, a blaze in the dark. A heavy branch swung low along the floor and, at the last moment, rose up sharply, catching Kip in the chest. His breath was forced out of him and he tumbled backwards into the gaping mouth of the well. Shadow grabbed for him as he flew through the air and was pulled along.

They plummeted through darkness, spinning as they fell. There was no air in Kip's lungs to muster a scream, just the total blackness surrounding them. The hissing of the tree limbs faded above until there was no noise at all.

Except the beating of drums.

9

Enos's back was to him, the sheet falling just at his waist. He raised his hand towards the shaft of sunlight that streamed in the window, letting it move between his fingers.

Kip smiled and linked his fingers with Eno's, capturing a small bit of light.

"The Academy said I can bring a guest, even a non-alchemist."

Especially a non-alchemist.

He wanted someone there that came from the real world, not a student of academies and houses. Not a cog in some antiquated wheel.

Kip's initiation ceremony was tomorrow. People would come to Academy Tower from all the great houses of the world to see one of their own ascend.

Enos turned to face him.

What had he said?

I wouldn't miss it.

Good.

Do I have to dress up?

Maybe a bit?

Do I get to learn any secrets?

Just a few.

Then they had stopped talking. Kip thought, *I know things end. I know, in theory, nothing is permanent, but surely this. Surely this.*

There was so much light now. The morning sun filled the window.

So much light.

The white light grew, and with it came a symphony.

It came out of the void. It grew steadily until it filled his field of vision. Even more than that, it was wider and bigger than anything he'd ever seen, like approaching the ocean for the first time. The music of the light was a chorus that crashed on him like waves. Closer and closer it came until it left his vision and filled his head, singing its sweet but overwhelming music.

Louder and louder and louder.

Kip opened his eyes.

The darkness was so complete he thought he'd been struck blind. He waved his hand in front of his face, looking for even a hint of light. There was the barest outline, so faint it was hard to be sure if it was there at all.

Tears stung his eyes.

He moved achingly, checking his body for injury in the darkness. If he'd fallen as far as it had seemed, surely he would have been killed. But he knew, without having to be told, that he had passed into another world. The ground he sat on was no more part of Alchemy House than the mountains on Mars.

Kip shifted, reached out his hands and found a rocky surface. He knew these stones, knew every crack and imperfection of them. It was the bottom of his well.

The stones made a wall. He crouched in front of it and found his fists, locked into two white muscles. He beat them against the unforgiving surface. One hit after another, and with each hit a cry. If he could just batter himself against this wall, give himself to it, kill himself with it.

"If I could just join Enos!" he screamed.

The words flew upwards, like a bat up a chimney, leaving silence behind.

Two lights ignited in the blackness, and Kip felt Shadow's eyes on him; two questioning orbs, and the thought, again, *What is this thing? Is it really a childlike shadow, or much more?*

The eyes studied him with deep intensity, assessing, judging maybe.

"Does Kip want to join Enos?" the creature asked.

Kip slumped back, resting on his legs. His back felt like it would break, his fists throbbed. He looked down at his knuckles. Blood flowed, seeping from dozens of cuts. It looked black in the half-light of Shadow's eyes.

"I don't know," Kip whispered. "I don't know anything. I should kill myself, rather than live alone in that house up there, rather than sleep in an empty bed, and never laugh again."

"Blood is traded for death," Shadow said, "in one way or another. Blood is the coin for the ferryman. Does Kip want to pay the ferryman?"

Kip thought he could smell the blood on his hands, the

coppery scent of life. He started to wipe his hands together, smearing the blood over his knuckles, turning his palms up, blood filling the lines on the white pads of flesh.

"Just answer this, Shadow," Kip said softly. "Is there a point to any of it? I don't pretend I'm asking any questions that haven't been asked a thousand times by greater minds than mine. But no one's answered them, have they? Not really. Socrates, Plato, Aquinas. I...I can't *not* know anymore."

"Alchemy is transmogrification," Shadow said.

Kip heard a voice in his head, half-Shadow's and half-someone else.

Recall the tria prima. *List them for me now.*

"Mercury, sulfur, and salt."

And what do they denote?

"Spirit, soul, and body."

Correct.

Shadow spoke. "Kip looks for death, doesn't he? Why?"

"Because...I have to find meaning. I have to find signs and symbols that give *life* meaning. If a black cat isn't bad luck; if a bird in the house doesn't mean death..."

Kip stopped, his eyes finding the ground.

"What then?" Shadow asked.

"Then it's all meaningless, isn't it? All random. Then there's no lifeline to the afterworld. No hope of seeing him again. And all of this was for nothing. You find a belief system, thinking it's done out of wisdom, after careful observation of the world."

Shadow made a remote purring sound deep in his throat. Kip had observed it before and knew it to be a sign of the creature's empathy. It soothed him.

"We look for meaning to give order." Kip held up his

hand and clenched his fist, blood dripping from the folds of skin. "To hold on tightly to a mad world."

Shadow raised his hand to match Kip's, opening his fist, splaying his short fingers and pushing their palms together.

"Can you even understand, Shadow? They say if you could teach a lion to speak English, we still wouldn't understand each other, so different are our experiences. You're a creature of the underworld, aren't you?"

"Shadow's from behind the veil, yes."

"So how can you understand these things?"

"Does Kip want to join Enos?" Shadow asked again, just as patiently as before.

Kip nodded.

"Blood pays for the passage."

Kip opened his hands again, marveling at the amount of blood there. There was so much in the human body, and yet so little. So little could be spent and still bring death.

He could see the red water in the Three Nymphs Fountain. There had been so much blood then, too. *So much blood.*

He looked at the curved stone wall of the well, illuminated by Shadow's eyes. He wondered how he could have willed this thing to exist, what gave him the right?

"Alchemy is transmogrification," he whispered, then placed his open palms against the stone. A pulse of light shown around the edges of the rock. It flared and rippled upward. A low rumble filled his ears.

A section of the wall moved away, each stone separating until they floated into a void beyond. There was a dizzying order to it, like watching a puzzle fly into place, each stone moving with purpose. Piece by piece they formed a bridge. It hovered over a blue-black chasm. The new construction snaked out of sight, wrapped in fog.

The path called to Kip, begging him to put one foot in front of the other; to cross into the unknown world beyond. He felt Shadow behind him, gently nudging the back of his leg. Kip placed a bloodied hand on the newly-made archway, and patted the stone gently.

Maybe I'm saying goodbye to Alchemy House, to the well, to London.

Maybe.

He crouched and grabbed the leather straps of his green bag, then slipped an arm inside each loop so that it hung from his back.

Kip took a tentative step forward.

He passed through a film of blue light hanging in the air. He could feel it pass *through* him, feel it touch every bit of him. It ran through his blood, snaking along veins, climbing inside bones, and invading every cell.

He had the sense that he was floating above himself, watching his entrance into this new world. Shadow pattered at his side, his smoky tail wagging back and forth.

The bridge stretched into the shadows, hovering over the blue-black chasm. The darkness was so vast that it overwhelmed the mind. It was too big to be afraid of. Still, it drew his attention with every step, and he wondered what it would be like to simply fall and meet it. Were there stars trying to break through that abyss, pinpoints of light trying to escape its gravity?

Shadow, maybe sensing the pull of the chasm, nudged Kip again.

"Don't look down," he whispered.

Kip risked a look behind and saw the column of the well, now broken at the bottom, stretching up into a gray sky, like a chimney. He thought of the voice and their hours of conversation and it seemed like a dream from another life.

The voice stood where I'm now standing, sharing its bizarre thoughts and questions. And now it's waiting for me, somewhere in this strange land.

The bridge began to merge with the land beyond, blending the well-stones into darker earth. They were on solid ground now, leaving the floating stones behind. The texture felt odd. It had an uneasy give to it as if even the ground were not fully-formed.

Images flashed beneath his feet; signs of life trapped in obsidian, blinking in and out of existence.

Their path sloped down into a shallow valley, surrounded by giant stones on either side. They reached up like massive ribs only half-excavated from the ground, some slumbering stone beast left under the earth. They moved between the shadows the stones cast.

Crossing a shadow was like entering a small patch of night. Kip thought he saw pale stars in the brief darkness, twinkling as part of some alien constellation.

"Something's wrong done here," Shadow said. "Can Kip feel it? Something's been agitated."

"I...I don't know. I don't what it's supposed to feel like."

"This place should be calm and quiet. But the energy here..."

Shadow stopped and placed an open palm on the nearest rock. Kip was sure he saw a blue pulse shoot away from the creature's hand, a small tongue of lightning rippling away.

"...it's all wrong. It's conflicted. Angry."

It was 'angry' in London too, angry outside Alchemy House. Blackmoor has done something. I've done something.

The path began to rise again, lifting to a flattened plain. The ground turned to crude stairs that looked like they were newly formed, pushed up by the shifting of the earth.

Their way was blocked by a wall of gray cloud. It was a silent hurricane. Lightning moved inside it but with no sounds of thunder. Darkness rolled and crashed.

The beating of drums.

The clouds gathered like black cloth, weaving layer after layer into a new shape. Kip caught a glimpse of a figure in the eye of the storm, arms outstretched. It was quickly obscured as a new shape took form.

At first only a silhouette, a perfect black cut-out. Then features began to appear. Two large blue eyes shone from its head. They swirled with thought, the threads of a mind weaving together.

I can finally see you, human boy. I can see you with human eyes.

Black horns emerged from its forehead, poking through the dark skin. There was a wisp of smoky white on its crown. It wavered like the trail of an extinguished candle.

A piece of Blackmoor.

The thing was wrapped in a cloak, more shadow than fabric. It pooled on the stone ground, moving with its own life, losing focus as it faded and reappeared.

This was his voice in the well, the ear that he'd poured his sorrows into night after night. The thing that knew all the intimate parts of him and had listened so greedily.

The thing that wanted to be alive.

It had taken Lord Blackmoor and wrapped him in a shroud.

"You've come," the thing said, a paper cut of a smile on its face. "You've transcended worlds to be here."

10

K ip climbed the last steps and stood on the landing before the creature. Shadow stayed a few paces back, peering at the apparition from behind Kip, his head popping out and back as if he couldn't bear to look.

The thing towered over them, smiling and smiling.

"Call me...Vorax," it said, as if the thought had just occurred to him.

Kip remembered Lord Blackmoor using the word.

"Latin?"

"Yes, Latin. It means to be 'gluttonous, voracious.' To eat greedily, swallow up, consume, gorge oneself. That is my aim and desire."

Still the smile.

Its voice moved in and out of Kip's head, half-spoken and half-thought.

To unhinge my jaw and consume every bit of the world, to feel its life running through me, over me.

"But come, this is not the place for such talk."

Vorax gestured, a wide sweep of his arm. Kip followed his direction and saw, for the first time, a full table setting. It had appeared under the gray sky, fully-formed, and all of it a mockery of Lord Blackmoor's dinner.

"Is this acceptable?"

Is this how it's done, Kip?

Everything was obsidian. A jet black table with ornate legs anchored to the ground, or absorbed by it; ebony-colored plates and dinnerware on its surface. The Plateau de Délices was made of thorny vines, tamed to hold the various foods on offer, all of them as black as the rest of the setting.

Kip approached the table.

He wants me to play his little game, he thought. *He wants to talk, to do what he thinks humans do.*

Kip took a seat in a thorn-backed chair at one end of the table as Vorax mirrored him, sitting at the opposite end. There were three goblets, their glass etched with a smoky blackness. They filled themselves as liquid flowed from the bottom of the glass.

Kip looked at the third place-setting to his right and knew it wasn't meant for Shadow, but for some new surprise, some new thing to endure. Shadow sensed the tension and gave a weak moan from his place at Kip's feet.

"Are we expecting another guest?"

Vorax smiled a head-splitting grin; black teeth in a black head.

"Only honored guests, my friend. Someone who has earned a place among us, someone who binds us together."

A shape appeared on the horizon, a simple hazy blotch. It moved with a steady but flat gate as if it struggled to find life. Step by step it came, and Kip felt his heart quicken. He wanted to escape. He would have given anything to run from the table and back to his well, to climb its stones and be safe again. This world was too big.

The form approached, birthed from the haze and shadows.

Enos stepped up to the table.

Kip's vision blurred. The world was a tunnel now and Enos was at the end of it. Everything else was a fog. He could hear the blood pulse through his head as it made its way to his eyes, enriching this vision before him.

Enos was robbed of all color. No red blush under his tanned cheeks, no glint of green in his eye. His hair, once like a raven's wings, was the color of ash.

This place has burned him out. Is this what death is? Kip thought.

"You may sit," Vorax said to the apparition.

Enos didn't sit so much as vaporize into his chair, standing one moment, then, in a swirl of shadow, sitting the next. He stared straight ahead, unseeing, unmoving, his hands folded in his lap.

There was so much for Kip to say. The words stacked one on top of the other until they crashed together, leaving him speechless. He settled on the simplest thing he could find.

"Hello, Enos."

But there was no response, just a silent gaze.

Vorax cleared his throat. Kip could be on him in a second, his hands around his neck. He hated how intimately this shade knew him, how naked he was under his stare.

Vorax sensed the threat and smiled.

"I know every piece of you, Master Kip. There's no need for such anger, such fanciful notions as revenge."

His smile faltered as something crept over his face. His hands gripped the table, black claws digging into the surface. His features boiled as he lost control.

Something lurked just beneath the surface. Kip caught a glimpse of it before Vorax buried it again. It was like looking through black ice; Lord Blackmoor incased in the dark folds of Vorax's body.

The creature composed himself.

"You don't approve?" he asked. "Hades was a gentleman, to be sure, but he lacked barbarism; he lacked the brutality of death. You don't let Persephone get away. You grab her by the throat and you squeeze."

"Winter all year long," Shadow whined quietly.

"Lord Blackmoor is the coal that will drive my engine. I've learned so much from him already. He feels different from you. Are you all so different? He wants to hurt people."

"And so do you."

The smile again. The black teeth and gray mouth.

"The Gods of Death are long since gone. I'll take my piece of it while I may. Death used to mean something, Master Kip. It used to have an agenda. It shaped the fortunes of man, directed the arc of history. What would Isolde have been without the death of Tristan, or Arthur without Mordred's embrace? What are men without death to smash themselves against?

"Now death is the stuff of blind chance, a gutter that consumes the living without purpose. A hero may die with the same carelessness as a serving wench. A child dies of plague; an infant of typhoid. These deaths mean nothing, they don't move the world, they don't incite great deeds or a noble history. In the coming century, do you know how many will be pulped meat, dragged beneath the wheels of death's handiwork?

"If I could walk with humans for a while, learn their wants, see the structure of your new world, I could see my place in it again. I could give meaning to all this."

"We both know what you want." Kip spit the words out. "You're no different than Lord Blackmoor. All the thought and eloquence, when all you really want is dominion, to leave this place and take your corruption to my world."

What does it feel like to be alive?

Vorax's eyes blazed, the blue burning so brightly that it turned to a hot white. Something that looked like pain filled the two orbs. There was a quick stabbing motion as his body mutated again, pushing out in all directions. The layers of Vorax peeled away like a desiccated cocoon to reveal the shape of Lord Blackmoor.

Was he trying to speak? His mouth moved feebly, the skin pulling oddly away from bone. Any words that would have come were quickly cut off as Vorax snapped back to life, encasing Blackmoor again. His mouth yawned as blackness filled it. The magician's eyes were masked by pools of blue.

Kip gave a sideways glance towards Enos. Did any of this affect him? His beautiful eyes, once so full of life, were dimmed to nothing; two black peach pit eyes. Kip thought he could hear a constant murmuring, almost mantra-like, coming from his lover, but he couldn't be sure.

He wanted to reach out his hand and feel the familiar folds of his palm, to hold him even if just for a second.

"There is only one thing to want," Vorax said. "One thing that I desire: the antidote for death, the elixir of life. The Soul of All Things.

"We're both children of the in-between now, Master Kip.

If I'm to transcend this world I'll need more than just shadows, I'll need flesh and bone. I'll need a vessel.

"You will stay here. You will make this liquid gold for me and I will transcend this place. It's what you've always wanted. You wished for this place, whether you knew what you wished for or not. This is the laboratory you dreamed of; a world of elements, of raw material to work with.

"Take your longing, all your pain, and spin it into reality."

Kip stared out at the horizon and saw a shard of silent lightning strike in the distance. He imagined the threads of light it would send across the ground and the scar it would leave. The way it would transform sand to glass, nature's own alchemy.

Vorax knew the map of his heart, who better? He'd communed with this thing and spilled all of his secrets.

"And why would I do this?" Kip asked.

"It's been the driving force of your life. To bring back your beloved." He gestured towards Enos who was sitting with his same eerie silence. "This is your moment. Blackmoor gets his wish, to know the secrets of death. I get to know the secrets of life. I get to wrap myself in the organic forms that you prize so highly. And you, you get your Enos. Raise the dead, Kip, raise the dead and realize your purpose."

An explosion of purple thundered over the horizon; a bubble of purple light, like an eruption that refused to fade after detonation. If Kip squinted, he could see some busy activity in its shape. The purple light was etched with movement, like tiny lightning strikes.

The sound of it caught up with them. It rolled over the gray landscape in waves.

Vorax cupped his hands together and then moved them outward. A golden sphere filled in the space. It had some inner-workings that were in constant motion, moving parts that were calculating something. It reminded Kip of a clock but not one made by men. He thought he could hear the dim sound of bells in its shape, bells waiting to ring out.

The creature gave it a push and it flew towards the horizon with tremendous speed, racing to join the purple light that seemed impossibly far away.

"What...what was that?" Kip asked.

"Something that will keep the time for us. Meet me there, on that purple shore, after the striking of the tenth bell. Bring me what I've asked for, what we both want, a cure for death."

Kip still protested.

"I...I don't have the skill, I wouldn't know where to begin."

"This realm will be an education. Perhaps you will pass, perhaps you will fail, but you have ten bells to do either." He stretched out his arm.

"Explore this Pale World and find what you seek."

There was nothing left to say to the creature. Kip looked down at Shadow, hoping for some input, but his friend stared back in silence.

"We're not without some civility here. A place will been made for you."

Vorax picked up a bell from the table, a thorny thing made of obsidian. Again Kip felt the echo of the real world. Hours ago, Blackmoor had reached for his own bell and set this doom in motion.

The creature rang the bell but it made no sound that Kip could hear. The gray clouds parted.

There was movement from every direction as small black forms slinked from the shadows, some walking straight out of the rocks, others pattering along in groups, coming over a hill or across a valley.

It was an army of Shadows.

Hundreds of searching eyes surrounded the table. Kip's Shadow let out a low whine and pulled himself closer to Kip, gripping his leg.

They were Shadows but not *his* Shadow. Their differences were slight, but they were there; eyes that were a hair farther apart, a wider mouth, a longer tail. They kept coming until a sea of them surged around the table, its waves rolling off into the distance.

There were familiar sounds; a soft purring, the clicking of teeth. They spoke in a hushed language that Kip couldn't understand.

These Shadows had one difference that eclipsed all the others. Instead of soft blue eyes, theirs were an angry purple.

Vorax stood.

He opened his mouth to speak, but another spasm struck him, shredding his form and then snapping it back together. Something roiled inside him and he swayed on his feet. There was an explosion and he split down the middle, shadow-flesh stripping back layer after layer. His center carved out, revealing his prisoner.

Lord Blackmoor stood like a mummy in a sarcophagus before tumbling forward. He collapsed into the dirt. His body smoked, covered with a thin film that quickly evaporated.

The old man looked even older, his skin grayed and etched with deep wrinkles. Bony fingers pulled in the dirt as if remembering how to grasp.

My god, Kip thought. *He's still alive.*

The strip of white hair on his brow had spread to cover the rest of his skull. With some effort he raised his head, looking up at Kip with watery eyes.

"I found your secret," he said, before falling unconscious.

11

"You...you left him alive?"

"I'm not a monster, Master Kip. You'll find I only take what I need. Besides, two heads are better than one. Lord Blackmoor can lend his own expertise to our little project. Perhaps he can find things you cannot."

The Shadows gathered around the old man. Raising his weakened body over their heads, they began to retreat.

Kip wondered where they would take him.

And me, where do I go in this new world? he thought.

As if in answer to his thoughts, Vorax spoke.

"Rest here for the night," he said, gesturing to something behind Kip.

He turned to see a house constructed behind him. Shadows ran over its surface, building as they went. Wood knitted together. Stone pushed from the ground.

Every detail was in place and it was all familiar.

A single black shingle that stood out in a sea of green ones, like a tiny entrance to a cave. The iron latches that held the shutters in place, their twisted shapes catching the light.

There was a rod-iron fence with a metal owl fused to the top of it, perched and waiting with watchful eyes. A stone path zig-zagged to the front door.

It was Enos's house.

A cottage just outside London. It sat between the city and the greater wild of the country, a doorway to a bigger world. Now it sat alone, a single marker in an empty world.

The house was a lost memory. He looked at the position of every chair and cushion, the baubles on every shelf. How could they seem so right, but also so alien?

The shade of Enos followed him, walking with silent steps.

Bookshelves lined every available wall. In-between the books were the small worlds he'd created, the pocket-sized armadas ready to brave the sea. There were easily two-dozen ships in bottles. Kip found them spread throughout the house like small jewels, nestled between Brontë and Dickens. He could imagine their sails flapping, the crew scrambling on deck, following barked orders. When he peered through the rippled glass he could practically see it, a tiny world unfolding just for him. He could smell the minute portions of brandy that an obedient crew were rewarded with, the frying of lard and bacon, the smell of gunpowder and smoke, the feel of canvas and oakum.

Enos would give a story to each one, weaving a tale for Kip. In this one, Lord Nelson was a hero; in that one Napoleon was dastardly.

Not all were about war. Some stories struck out at new horizons, their tiny passengers longing for escape, longing to find some tropical wind that would blow them to someplace safe and warm.

Captain Currant in a first-rate three-masted cruiser looked for treasure.

Princess Katoomba wanted safe harbor after stealing the crown of Peter the Great.

Kip and Enos sailing to find the Floating Library of Antilla.

The fire in the hearth cast its glow, a setting sun reflected in each bottle.

He turned to find Enos, to see if he was as alive as his models. The gray shade lingered in the doorway, his eyes drawn to the fire and nothing else.

Kip walked up the stairs, testing the weight of every step beneath him. His feet led the way without any thought, pulling him left then right, until he entered the bedroom.

There was a book on the nightstand. Its spine cracked as he opened it and began to flip through the pages. All empty. One blank parchment after another flipped by his face. He was sure he'd been reading a book with words the last time he'd been here, but he couldn't remember now. *What had the words been? What did it matter?*

As the light dimmed outside, Kip felt the weight of his exhaustion. He tried to remember all the events that had come before this moment, but found it took an intense concentration. Snatches of memory rose to the surface.

Lord Blackmoor's smiling face that tipped towards a sneer.

The cold of space as it gripped Fairfield and Britten.

The attack on Alchemy House.

And Vorax.

Why was he forgetting?

Questions could wait. Kip pulled back the covers of Enos's bed and began to undress, letting his clothes fall to the floor in a heap. He looked down at his body and was startled by how gaunt he looked, too much bone where there should have been fat. Another skeleton for the underworld.

The Pale World.

He sat on the mattress and thought his body would sink through it, wrapped in comfort, and continue to fall, not caring how far down it went.

Kip looked up at Enos, who was standing stock-still by the door to the room.

"Join me," Kip said. "Let's sleep."

Enos made no move.

"Don't you want to? It could be...like it was."

Some unseen thing caught Enos's attention and he looked at the blank wall to his right, staring like a cat at some mystery that humans couldn't see. Kip rose from bed and crossed the room. He approached Enos timidly until he was standing in front of him.

"Enos," he whispered, trying to get his attention.

He turned his head back and caught Kip's eye for the briefest moment. Then looked ahead, straight through him.

He doesn't see me.

Kip rested his arms on Enos's shoulders. There was barely any form to him, just the small push-back on Kip's palms. Any more pressure and he thought his hands would pass straight through him.

"I've missed you, Enos. I've missed you so much. I didn't think I could miss anything so much. I thought there would always be laughter, that it would fill the house, bounce off of every wall. Did you miss me?"

Enos's eyes, robbed of color, focused on some horizon Kip couldn't see. It was like looking into a nearly frozen pond, a barrier forming over the world below. And just as cold.

Kip wrapped his arms around the shade, only the suggestion of body there to rest on. He found the crook of Enos's neck and buried his face there.

No warmth. No scent.

"Didn't you miss me, Enos?"

Kip barely slept that night. This version of Enos's house was a tomb, just a place for dead things to decay. He tossed and turned, occasionally spying a bolt of silent lightning out the window, striking somewhere out in the darkness. The flash of light lit the room and he turned to see Enos, still standing by the door; immovable.

A deafening sound cracked the air.

Kip nearly screamed. He rolled from the bed naked, his hands up to protect himself from any assault. The peeling gong of a bell thundered over the horizon, coming in waves that mixed into an echoing loop. Beneath the sound was the familiar beating of drums, each heavy beat played by some angry god.

Kip tripped into his clothes, stepping into his pants as he hopped across the floor. He turned to look for Enos but there was no sign of him.

The sky dimmed outside as a vast star-scape opened up. It vibrated with the chiming clock, the pinprick stars blazing with each gong. The depths of space stretched out in all directions; heavenly bodies whirled and smashed together in slow motion. This was no map Kip had ever seen, alien constellations weaving their patterns above.

Pale gray light absorbed the star-scape and then spread out, covering the horizon. It was dawn.

Kip heard the scratching of claws along the outside of the house. Dozens of Shadows criss-crossed past the window, stippling the light as they sped past. He could hear them furiously working, ripping at the structure.

They're taking it apart, he realized. *They're disassembling this memory.*

The floor heaved, floorboards cracking then falling away. A hole broke through the wall as two purple-orb eyes peered in for a moment before moving on.

Shadow, his Shadow, bounded into the room, hopping over the disappearing floor. He went pale as a piece of the wall gave way, passing through him, then snapped back into focus.

"Time to go!" he yelped.

Kip grabbed the rest of his clothes, rolling them into a bundle, then snatched up his green satchel and turned towards the door. The house heaved to the right and Kip and Shadow went with it, hitting the eastern wall as picture frames rained down on them. The corner of one caught Kip in the temple and a thin trail of blood bloomed there, dripping down the side of his face.

The bed was sliding towards them now, vibrating over the decaying floor, looking like some bucking animal. Kip scooped up Shadow and ran towards the door. The bed sped past them and crashed through the wall, raining splinters into the air and smashing the remaining pictures.

Memories, Kip thought. *Memories can't hurt you.*

But he knew they could.

The staircase was now an abstraction, impossible to navigate. Kip reached out for a bannister that was no longer anchored to the floor. It wobbled then came apart, falling a story down to the ground below.

The Shadows continued their work, like a host of termites. More eyes and claws sped past as they dissolved the house.

The floor of the balcony heaved again as it decoupled from the rest of the house. It floated in mid-air, balanced on two support beams and began to fall. Shadow leaped forward, going pale as he found a dark patch nestled along one of the beams. He snaked down to the ground floor below.

"Slide down!" he purred.

Kip jumped forward as the floor fell away, and rode the beam down to the living room below. He landed with a *thud* and rolled across the floor as splinters fell like rain.

The bookshelves heaved as more purple light broke through. Books fell around them, empty pages fluttering by. They knocked the bottled ships onto the floor where the glass shattered, freeing the tiny vessels.

His mind filled with nonsense. He wanted to be on one of those ships, sailing away from here on a sea of broken glass.

Shadow was tugging at his sleeve, hopping up and down on his small legs. A rending *crack* above made them run, jumping through the front door as the structure collapsed, bits of wood and tangled roots snapping at their heels.

They ran past the wrought-iron fence with the faulty latch, slamming it wide.

The Shadows moved over the surface of the wreckage like the tide over sand, their purple eyes blurring into a spiral of light as they sucked up all that remained of Enos's home. A piece of Enos was going with it, a puzzle-piece of memory that had kept him intact in Kip's mind. As if to cement the thought, the pale vision of Enos joined them, standing stone-still to watch the Shadows do their work. He was even more faint now than the day before.

The earth yawned and reclaimed the house, leaving a swirl of dust, and then nothing. The Shadows stood over the empty space, lost in a trance-like state. Then, one by one, they retreated.

All that remained was the bit of metal fence. The owl watched them, left on his lonely perch. *That will be gone soon enough,* Kip thought.

Through the arch of the fence Kip could see a faint path, no more than a layer of dust. It snaked over the horizon and out of sight, drawn to the purple cloud on the horizon.

Kip had no doubt the path would take them there. But what they would meet on the way, he didn't know.

12

This world is growing as I inhabit it.

Kip's senses were filled with the Pale World. It was ever-evolving, shrugging off the dream and becoming real.

The smooth ground had changed. Black roots snaked from the earth like wet eels gathered together for warmth. They all moved along the same path.

Kip looked back to see Enos trailing behind. He seemed incapable of walking with them no matter how slowly they moved. The light pierced his body like sunlight cutting through smoke.

It was painful to see him so diminished.

If this world is coming into focus, perhaps he will, too.

Shadow had his nose to the ground, his attention captured by something Kip couldn't see. He'd read that some animals had such a keen sense of smell that it became a kind of second sight. His friend looked up at a wall of mist ahead.

"Trees," he purred in his sing-song voice.

Massive dark columns stretched towards the sky, their

tops hidden by fog. Branches bent over the path like meshed fingers. It looked like the nave of a cathedral. Kip wondered what he'd find at the altar.

A cool breeze flowed down the path and then reversed, like a giant breathing.

There was a shape moving through the trees, far down the trail.

Kip doubted if he'd even seen it, until it appeared again. It weaved between the trees as it moved in stuttering bursts. The mist moved with it like a cloak.

Shadow stood on his hind-legs peering down the path. His eyes were wide and alert.

"Can you tell what it is?" Kip whispered, hating how his voice sounded in the gloom.

His friend put a paw to the ground and a splinter of blue raced away from it. It was weaker than before but still visible. It ran down the path in a zig-zagging pattern.

Shadow's eyes pulsed with its movement. But whatever he'd done, it returned no answer.

Kip thought he could name the shadow: Lord Blackmoor.

Vorax said he'd taken what he needed from the magician, a cocoon feeding on the butterfly inside instead of giving it strength. The old man had gotten a head-start, moving under the cover of night. Even when broken, a man so powerful could be dangerous. There was no use chasing him.

What would I do if I caught him?

As the trees closed in, a foggy light began to mark the trail. The hollows in the trunks held soft green lights.

They look like street-lamps.

The trees parted, as they entered a clearing.

A bulge in the earth rose slightly into a small mound, speckled moss covering it in patches. The roots all converged to this center point and poured into a tree at the top of the hill.

Kip moved closer.

It looked as if gravity had compacted it, not allowing it to flourish. The fingers of each limb had grown into small cages, wood knitting together to form bars. They were clamped shut with no locks or hinges, no way for their captives to escape.

Huddled in each cage was a black bird, more shadow than real. They moved in a blur, their smoky wings trying to expand but hitting the walls of their cages. Some pecked at the wood with needle beaks. Each looked out with sharp blue eyes, cocking their heads to the side to observe Kip and Shadow. Harsh bird calls cut the air.

Kip thought of the bird woman of Potter's Market and her caged birds. Only those, for a price, could be set free. Each of these had a life sentence.

The trunk was deformed, the gnarls and knots flowing together; a face made of bark, cracked wood forming a mouth with splintered lips. Two eyes were sunken into the tree, mercifully closed.

Please don't open, Kip thought, but knew they would. This world had things to reveal and nothing could stop that now.

With a wooden creak the eyes came to life, two watery pools of green, like some frosted plant matter before a thaw.

"Magic Boy..." the tree rasped, and the wooden face of Ragman came into focus. The bark and lichen moved with the words as the croaking voice came out. It was a voice in constant pain.

"Alchemy Boy," Shadow corrected helpfully.

"Ahhhhhhh, yes. I'd almost forgotten. All your potions and fires and experiments. Things get forgotten down here. All I remember is a street corner somewhere, a vague point on a map. Perhaps I stood there once and talked to passers-by.

"There's a house too, a darkened house and trees. So many trees, swarming around me, hunting for me. Do you remember these things?"

"I...I remember," Kip said.

"And a pulling and rending."

"I remember that too."

"Good," the tree sighed, "I thought I'd gone mad. It's easy to go mad. It requires the slightest push, a nudge even."

A warbled chorus filled the air from above. It had words in it, but only just.

"Magic Boy! Magic Boy!"

The cawing of a hundred caged birds, the words blending with the sound of beating wings. Kip backed away from the tree, overcome by the sound, wishing it would stop.

Enos stood a few paces away, as calm as ever, unmoved by anything before him. The birds settled in time and returned to their muted squawking.

"Do you like my chorus, boy?"

"No, I don't like it. I don't like anything down here."

"Do you like gold? There's gold down here, to be sure. I can feel it coursing in my roots, tiny filaments of it spreading to every limb and bud.

"Do you want to be planted here, in this forest? We all return to the earth, boy. It consumes us in the end. The world that hides from us as we build over it, it returns in full force. Fungi and rot, insects, rust; all so hungry for every bit that we have to offer.

"I'm part of it now, and a beggar no more. I don't need your alms, your coins, your baubles. You can have them."

The Ragman tree gave a hacking cough and something dropped to the ground. tumbling past his wooden lips. It gleamed in the soft dirt, brilliant by contrast like some lost jewel in the night. It was Shadow's medal, the medal he'd offered in place of money.

He heard Shadow make a small sighing sound as if he were seeing this treasure for the first time. *Is he forgetting, too?* Kip thought.

Shadow scurried forward to grab the shining bit of metal. He turned it over in his paws, letting it catch the light.

"No need for earthly things here, true as true," Ragman said. "You can have them all."

With that, the tree began to shake. First a flutter of movement in the upper branches. It alarmed the dark birds caged there. They squawked and screamed, chattering in their hidden language. Their eyes flared, filling the branches with a pale glow.

Ragman's face contorted, becoming even more tree-like, if that were possible. The wood that made up his cheeks and brow cracked, like dried driftwood.

The trunk was swaying and shaking now. Shining veins surfaced from the ground, running up the length of the tree. *It's metal*, Kip realized. He saw the mix of silver, copper, and gold as Ragman drew it from the soil.

Shadow cocked his head to one side as he backed away, still clutching his recovered prize.

Then came the sound. The deafening tolling of Vorax's bell. Just as before, it sent a ripple over the earth, reality faltering for a moment. The sky opened up above them, a swirling galaxy rotating, and piercing starlight looking down like a million eyes.

Kip heard a voice break through the din of the bell but he couldn't decipher the words. It was high-pitched and breathless. He wanted to answer it but didn't know what to say.

The sound of the bell rolled into the familiar drumbeat.

Boom. Boom. Boom.

The drums faded, leaving a laughing Ragman behind. His choked voice was nearly unintelligible. It was the voice of a tree cracked by lightning.

"You can't buy more time, Magic Boy. Not with all the alms in the world. Not with every bit of charity there is."

The tree's wooden jaw unhinged and a flood of coins came out, spewing onto the ground, bouncing off each other and skidding across the earth. They pelted Kip's feet as he looked on in horror. Every coin from a beggar's lifetime, returned.

Kip looked for Enos and saw him calmly walking away, continuing down the forest path as if he were taking a stroll on a sunny day.

The Ragman tree heaved to one side as its roots punched through the ground, searching for Kip and Shadow. It broke the spell they were under and they turned and ran, bolting down the path that Enos had taken.

With another rending *crack*, the earth began to split, snaking fissures all vomiting coins and bits of metal, stripping the earth of all its elements. Every bird was screaming now. Kip looked back to see some crushed in their cages. Shadowy feathers rained down.

Ragman's laughing voice trailed them.

The fissures became chasms, each one spewing metal

from deep underground. They ran down the path as uprooted trees followed. Shadow went pale as he ducked beneath grasping roots and over unsteady ground.

A cliff face rose ahead, a towering wall that blocked their way. There was a doorway carved into the stone, its arched frame rising overhead. It led into the mountainside.

Their one route of escape.

Ashen roots tore from the ground and wove together to block the entrance. He could see the wood squeezing together like a vice, sheering bark away.

Kip's breath came in choked waves. He turned to see a roiling forest of roots and branches coming towards them. One tree towered over the others; the Ragman Tree. The river of coins and metals flooded every open space.

Sublimation, Kip thought, *the turning of a solid into a gas; the freeing of an element.*

He threw his bag to the ground and searched through the contents. His mind fogged once again, struggling to find what had once come so easily. His bag felt foreign, like looking through someone else's luggage.

Shadow compacted to a ring of black around Kip and spun in a dizzying circle, chipping away at the searching trees and flood of metal, but slowly losing the battle.

"Kip must hurry!" his voice boomed.

Kip's hurrying, Kip thought, *as fast as he can.*

A vial fell into his palm and he knew it was the right one, a forgotten thing suddenly remembered. He uncorked it and gave it a quick sniff to confirm. The acrid smell burned his lungs and watered his eyes.

"To my side, Shadow!"

His friend reformed and clung to his leg as the entire forest moved to fill the gap. Kip poured the contents of the vial around them in a perfect circle. The effect was immediate. The coins and metals were released from their form, hissing into vapor as they crossed the circle. A brilliant-colored smoke sprung into the air, intense violets and greens with flashes of blue. The tree limbs that touched the gas recoiled as their bark exploded into the same toxic cloud. The tree branches that blocked the doorway quivered and then retreated.

The Sublimation Tonic began to fade, boring into the ground and then evaporating. The tree limbs roiled again, ready to close in. The ground heaved behind them as the lumbering form of the Ragman Tree approached, its upper branches swaying, the caged birds screeching as they were battered against their wooden bars.

"Am I an Alchemist now, Magic Boy?" the tree roared, splinters of wood falling from his face. His deep green eyes were livid, two daggers that would have pierced Kip if they could.

The cages contracted, like tightening fists, releasing a new peal of shrieks from the birds. Kip looked away, squinting his eyes, but heard the sound of crushed bone and flesh. Black wispy feathers rained down on them, landing in Kip's hair.

He slipped his hand into his bag once again, his fingers scrambling over the contents, as Ragman's ruined faced leaned in. A cold breath came from the hollow of the tree, rising through his mouth and over thorny teeth.

Kip thrust his palm forward, coated in the Fixation powder. It burst into flame. Searing bolts gouged Ragman's eyes. They burst like two ripe fruits and their hollows sucked up the flame. It entered the wooden shell of his body, igniting it from the inside.

The blue flame shone through cracks in the trunk, streaks of light running up and down the tree and growing in intensity. The fire spread through the forest, finding the network of roots that connected the trees. Geysers of flame vented through the ground in sharp bursts, springing up in random patches like fireworks.

Ragman screamed, and Kip matched his scream as the fire started to burn his flesh. In that moment he wanted to burn the world, to make this a place of ash and dust. He wanted his fire to cover the land, to find his well and burst into London, flow down streets, squeeze through alleyways. *Hurt for hurt*, he thought. *Only that would set things right.*

He gasped from the thought and from the pain that came with it, then drew his hand away and turned to the blocked tunnel.

Deeper we go.

"Deeper we go," Shadow said. They nodded at each other and Kip extended his hand again, the fire blinding them both. The web of branches finally abandoned their guard, and pulled away from the tunnel, snaking up the rock face.

The inferno that was Ragman lunged towards them, ready to smash them with his last act, like a burning ship run aground. Kip and Shadow leapt through the tunnel entrance and ran down the passage way, not daring to look back. Kip let the fire in his hand go out, his flesh pink and stripped.

The tree collided with the tunnel; a great calamity of sound and vision. Ragman's last scream blended with the roaring fire. It melted the rock behind them, sloughing off the tunnel entrance, glowing red like a lava flow.

Kip didn't dare look back, even as the heat seared his back and cut his shadow into the floor of the stone tunnel.

There was a final rending sound and the smell of charred wood, its odor wafting up the tunnel.

Autumn. Burning wood, a stoked hearth. To be safe again, to be comfortable and content.

The fire died behind them as they ran, burnt to nothing and leaving only darkness.

13

They ran blindly in a pitch black world. Kip had his hands out in front of him, feeling for some surface to grab onto. The side of the tunnel scraped against his knuckles and he called out in pain as he felt the warmth of blood on his skin. But there was no time to process it.

The floor of the tunnel fell away.

Kip was airborne. There was a moment of vertigo as he thought he'd taken flight. Maybe he would sail straight through the darkness and find light on the other side. Instead he tumbled forward and hit unyielding rock, slick with water. The tunnel flew by at a dizzying speed.

Wet roots grabbed at them, pulling skin and clothing. His hand, still burning, was a dim light in the dark. Shadow moved in a spiral next to him, sometimes sliding, sometimes running along the wall, his blue eyes nearly vibrating.

A final, explosive howl from behind bounced down the tunnel until it was all around them, an echo doomed to repeat forever. A flare of orange light became visible for a moment until their descent left it behind.

Streams of water ran over the stone, speeding their fall.

Kip was sure they'd be dashed to pieces by some immovable surface below, his bones shattering in a heap.

What if I fell forever? Down and down, past all the foundations of this world, past whatever was beyond that.

And then it was over.

The tunnel leveled out and they slid to stop.

Water had collected in shallow pools along the floor, no bigger than puddles. They looked like tidal pools left by a retreating ocean. Each pool had pinpricks of green light that winked in and out of sight, small universes rotating in black water.

Shadow was face down in one of them. He raised his head then shook it violently, beads of water catching the blue from his eyes.

Kip heard his own breathing, trapped in the tightness of the tunnel. His heart raced as he thought of the tons of rock above him, miles of it for all he knew. He had to put a hand to his chest to calm himself.

"Are you okay, Shadow?" His voice was an echo.

"Shadow thinks we've done this before."

He was right. It was a dim echo of what had happened before they'd come to the Pale World.

Ragman had attacked them and they'd escaped through a hearth.

Through a tunnel.

And fallen into darkness.

Into a well.

And landed in an unknown world.

"Maybe Vorax isn't too creative. Or maybe it's some sort of purgatory."

"What's purr-gate-story?"

"It's an in-between place where someone has to live out their sins over and over again."

"Is it a real place?"

"I don't think so."

"Good."

Kip got to his feet slowly, testing the height of the tunnel. It was just high enough for him to stand.

"Should we go forward?" he asked his friend.

Shadow purred softly and padded ahead.

They walked in silence as Kip listened for any sound. The quiet was suffocating. It was a kind of peacefulness that could drive you mad. There was no noise for distraction or to find your bearings, just an unending hush.

He reached his hand out to steady himself against the wall of the tunnel, and to remind himself that it was still there; that they were still anchored to a reality, no matter how strange. The stone that ran under his fingers was chilled and slightly damp. The only light was the dim projection of Shadow's eyes as they bobbed in the darkness and cast two weak pools of blue on the floor.

Kip thought of using his Fixation solution, but his hand was too sore now. He heard the echo of his footsteps along the stone floor and the excited staccato of Shadow's feet next to his.

When his mind had any breathing room, Enos would find him. The thought of him always showed up uninvited. He wondered if his shade was here in the darkness, silently guiding them, or if he had gone ahead.

The sound of a muffled explosion pulled him from his

daydream. There was some great and destructive work taking place down the tunnel. They heard its echo like rolling thunder coming from ahead. It sounded like the beating of drums. Shadow stopped and put his head to the floor, a blue halo of light spreading onto the stone.

"What do you hear?"

"Trouble maybe...maybe not."

The booming quieted and they moved on, creeping in the blackness.

Kip thought his eyes were playing tricks as a soft pink light filled the tunnel. It flooded over the stone, drawing out strange angles and the glint of minerals. It grew stronger as they walked until it was joined by new colors, purple and blue playing in the pink.

The ground opened up beneath them, falling away into a bottomless cavern, an untapped mine filled with rich veins of color. The rock below glowed with shifting hues. Strands of white traced upwards like small lightning strikes moving up from the depths.

The earth looked wounded, like the foundation of the Pale World had been laid bare for them. Kip felt a shifting vertigo as he looked down. He imagined jumping into the pit below, free-falling into the heart of it.

Down and down into the endless.

"What is this place, Shadow?"

"Kip's not the only one with a well. Everything has its origin."

A flash of purple glinted in Shadow's eyes, but if it was a reflection from below or something else, Kip couldn't be sure. Shadow fixed the medal to his chest. How it stayed there, Kip didn't know, but it was a part of him now. Even if it was just an artifact pulled from a drawer in Alchemy House.

There were other artifacts from Alchemy House, Kip thought, and his mind suddenly raced.

He dropped to his knees, sliding his bag from his shoulders again and opening it. As if magnetized, his hand went to one of the inner pockets of the bag and found a thin circle of metal there.

He pulled out Enos's bracelet.

Maybe this world was the catalyst that would make things possible. All his failed attempts to call Enos in the real world might be amplified here, in the world that was being created around them.

Holding the bracelet in his mouth, he searched for the proper tools, removing a small copper plate and two vials; one with liquid, one with powder, their glass catching the light of Shadow's eyes.

Kip lay the plate on the floor and poured two drams of the liquid onto its surface, He pulled the cork from the second bottle with a *snap* and sprinkled the powder over the liquid. It smoked immediately, a dancing wick of light crawling upwards.

Kip cradled the bracelet in his hands, like a secret he wasn't ready to reveal. The process would mean losing this artifact forever. But it was a trade that would be worth it; an artifact for the real thing.

A sacrifice to move forward.

He placed it over the plate and let it drop into the active mixture there.

A blaze of metallic light seared his eyes, dazzling him with white circles and lines. Designs clashed in the flames, destroying themselves only to be reborn.

The experiment activated the cavern below. Illuminated veins of minerals in the rocks made a network of color. They formed patterns that seemed too precise to be random. It was like the ancient art of cave paintings, as if some primitive people had designed all of this eons ago.

A steady breeze pumped up from the depths, tangling in Kip's hair. It had a voice, a droning mutter. Kip thought he could hear echoes of Vorax in it.

What does it feel like to be alive?

The bracelet burned down to nothing, smoking and cracking, as a small sigh issued from it. The metal liquefied and ran into the fire. It met with a wave of sparks. The mine below turned from pink to blue, bathing them in its light.

"It's mercury," Kip whispered. "Pure mercury encased in the metal."

Shadow studied it, watching the gray metal flow with its alien motion as it slithered into the flames, finding the bedrock below before it evaporated. Then something else was born.

A delicate pinpoint of light rose from the degraded metal, no more than a whisper. It bobbed lazily upwards floating between Kip and Shadow, winking like a star.

"It's the anima of mercury. The animating principle of it. It's been released."

It was Shadow's turn to whisper. "Catch it, Kip. Catch it."

Kip reached into his bag and pulled out an empty vial. He brought his hands up like he was chasing a firefly, cupping them around the small light. Gently letting it find its own way, he nudged it towards the open mouth of the vial. It filled the glass vessel with its light, expanding into its new home as Kip quickly corked the top.

The two marveled at the small thing and knew it held some meaning. Surely it would be revealed to them. As his friend watched, Kip thought he saw a sliver of purple cut across the blue of his eye again. It moved so quickly he wondered if he'd even seen it.

Rather than putting the vial back in his bag, Kip tucked it into his pocket. He was met with a splinter of pain as his palm brushed against a sharp object. Carefully he pulled it out. It was the shard of Sulfur Glass he'd hurriedly stowed there.

Kip turned it in his hand, ignoring the tear of blood that dripped to the ground. The glass was an inert black surface. It caught the light in the tunnel with its oily sheen.

He held it up to his eye, peering into an ebony mirror. Maybe it would show him an echo of the world he'd come from, or the final sight before it had shattered, the torment of Lord Blackmoor over the well.

At first there was nothing. It was like looking through a darkened window, trying to spy the abandoned interior inside. Slowly, images began to gather. They knitted together from strands of light.

See now, the world you left behind.

And he did see. The vision came to him, unfurling black smoke that danced and slithered into shape.

He was in his well, only moving upwards instead of down. He sped out of it, past his laboratory, through the hearth, pulling back to a familiar world. The tower of Alchemy House appeared and then the image sped outwards, showing the street corner where it sat, cloaked in darkness. It looked decrepit, robbed of something that had been there before.

Then Kip saw the branches pushing outwards, escaping from every shingle and windowpane. They cracked the sidewalk as they were birthed from his basement and laboratory. The shadow of trees were cast over everything, twisted limbs that cracked through paving stones, and snaked around lampposts, choking out their light. He imagined the well bubbling like a cauldron, brewing up the ashen limbs that now groped like fingers, always searching.

But what were they searching for?

There was a sound like a wind moving through an open door, and Kip felt the chill that came with it.

"Tell me what you see, boy," a voice said in the darkness.

Kip jumped to his feet and spun around to face it.

Two red glints appeared across the chasm of the mine. They bobbed like fireflies as the figure walked forward. Kip didn't need to see who it was, the voice was forever imprinted into his mind; Lord Francis Blackmoor.

"Is that the world now, the one spied through your glass? Or is this the real one? One of them is a dream, boy."

"You're still limping on, Blackmoor?"

Is there a smile beneath the red eyes?

"I left last night, before the tolling of that accursed bell. I crept through the forest while it slept. Anything to get away from Vorax and his Shadows. Whatever he did to me, it continues. This place is feeding on me. Why are you untouched by it?"

The magician waved his hand, not wanting an answer.

"No matter."

His voice was filtered through the magic, warping it into an inhuman sound. The light from the mine shone on his face now, highlighting the deep wrinkles and wasting that Vorax had left behind.

"Do you like my handiwork, Master Kip?" he said, gesturing to the cavern below. It reacted to his presence, turning a deep red. "I mined the depths looking for answers, laying open the flesh of the Pale World. I should have known you'd come along.

"You move from one dark place to the next, don't you? Crawling on your belly back to your basement, or this approximation. Anything to slink back to safety."

His red eyes pulsed as he spoke, the light growing stronger.

"You're a murderer. Who cares what you think," Kip said. "I ought to kill you right now."

The magician laughed at that, far too amused.

"From all the way over there?"

The magician stretched his hands out, palms up, his fingers curled into claws. The mine began to close, thrashing with light as it filled in. Sparks shot up from the depths, bouncing off stone and leaving comet tails of color. A bridge formed between them, the stone turning to a dead gray again. The last bit of the cavern closed around them with the finality of a slammed door. They were in the darkness again, except for Blackmoor's glowing red eyes.

"You think you could contend with me? Fairfield and Britten might have a different opinion. All their knowledge and experience couldn't save them. It's one thing to have learned, and quite another to have practiced. A book is a weak rebuttal to a knife.

"Vorax tasked us with finding the Soul of All Things, each in our own manner. So work your little parlor tricks, boy. I have other designs on this place."

The red blazed.

"Designs that don't include you."

Blackmoor thrust a fist out and hammered the wall to his right. A grinding sound came from where his knuckles met the stone and he began to recite an incantation, his breathy mumbling echoing in the closeness of the tunnel.

Shadow ran between Kip's legs, his shape rippling in the darkness, and charged towards Blackmoor. The magician didn't move. He didn't see the world around him.

Shadow jumped, his clawed fingers stretching towards his prey, a black mass roiling around him.

A column of stone punched out from the wall and knocked Shadow off balance. He hit the opposite side of the tunnel with a *thud* and slid down the wall. Shards of stone crisscrossed in front of Blackmoor, dilating to a narrow opening, leaving only his laughing face exposed. He'd made a wall between them. Kip's side was in constant motion, the stone rippling like a living thing. Fissures formed under Kip's feet as some tectonic shift occurred.

The tunnel closed around Kip and Shadow as Blackmoor watched.

"Buried alive," he said, smiling. "Can you die in the Pale World, or will you be entombed here?"

The barrier of stone he was behind closed completely, his red eyes and trailing laughter the last thing to disappear.

Kip had no time to think. He shuffled through his bag, his mind racing but finding no answers. A column of stone punched down from the ceiling and he darted out of the way, a hair's breadth from having his head caved in.

The only light was the soft glow of Shadow's eyes. He'd scampered back to Kip's feet.

"What do we do?" his friend asked.

Kip didn't know. How could he possibly know.

A wall of stone hit has back and slid him forward just as the opposite wall moved towards them.

Shadow expanded again, darting around the shrinking cavern as he tried to push back against it.

With a sudden *crack* beneath their feet, Kip felt the rush of something cold. Beyond cold, it was nearly frozen. Icy water rushed over his feet and quickly climbed to his ankles. He reached down and dipped his finger in the liquid and then brought it to his tongue.

Salt water.

A mad hope overtook him.

Kip shuffled through his bag in the dark, the water now at his thighs.

"I need to call the water forward. I need to strengthen it," he said.

Shadow seemed less convinced.

"The water seems pretty strong already."

Not strong enough.

A mason jar brushed against his searching hand and he gripped it, feeling the familiar edges. Pulling it out, he removed the cap, as a strong and familiar odor hit him. There was no time for measurements or caution. He tilted the jar, spilling the contents into his hand and then dusted the mixture around him in a circle.

A flare of blue light moved outward, like a ripple from a stone dropped in still water. The whirlpool around them exploded with a new force, spinning them in their ever-shrinking cavern. Kip put his hands up and pushed back against the lowering ceiling as the water reached his neck.

The strengthened water punched a hole in the rock below with another loud *crack*. The water level began to drop, tugging at them as it tried to pull them with it. Kip reached into his bag again, finding the pockets sewn into the walls of the bag, and found what he was looking for.

It was a small hardened ball, no bigger than a marble. Solidified oxygen.

Kip shouted to Shadow over the tumult.

"Do you need oxygen to live?"

"Nah!" his friend replied, as if he'd been offered nothing more than a cup of tea.

"Okay!"

Kip tucked his arms into the loops of his bag, securing it onto his back, then popped the ball into his mouth. As soon as it hit his saliva it began to fizz, the bubbles racing across his tongue and down his throat, some flying up his nose.

"Let's go!" he said, his voice a bubbling distortion.

The water tugged at him furiously, the larger hole creating a vortex that wanted to drag him under. Letting go of the rocks that had nearly encased him, he let the water take him down.

Kip was thrown into a frigid world of pitch black. The water rushed into his ears and stung his skin as it battered him, spinning him in circles until he lost all direction. He heard the muffled sound of the tunnel's final collapse above and felt a wave of bubbles wash over him as the cavern expelled its final breath.

In a panic, he looked for any sign of Shadow and then spotted his orb-eyes, bouncing like two jellyfish in the dark. They came closer. A tiny pawed hand tugged at Kip's sleeve. Shadow had picked a direction and who was Kip to argue? Salt water meant the sea, and if the sea had gotten in, there would have to be a way for it to get out.

A trail of fizzing bubbles streamed from Kip's mouth and nose as he kicked forward, his eyes on Shadow.

He didn't dare look down; didn't dare contemplate the open space below and what might be in it. Giant creatures of the deep sea filled his mind, their needle teeth and dead eyes coming towards him, their patience as they waited for new prey.

Sea monsters to attack Enos's bottled ships.

Kip swam forward, his mind on his arms and kicking legs.

How long would solidified oxygen last? He couldn't remember how long it had bubbled and boiled in his experiments, always so safe and controlled. It had never had a living thing sucking at it for life.

The current that had pushed into the cavern now looped around and moved in the opposite direction, an inhale turning into an exhale. They followed the breath, all feeling leaving Kip's limbs. His bag scrapped along the rocky ceiling above him and he imagined he could still hear the rumble of collapsing stone as Blackmoor's magic filled in the tunnel.

The oxygen ball had shrunken to the smallest tablet as it bounced around inside his mouth. The bubbles were coming in starts and fits now. Soon it would be used up.

Shadow swam ahead, slowly expanding the distance between them.

Then it appeared, not a monster or leviathan, but the outline of Enos. He floated ahead of Kip, untouched by the water as he occupied some different space. Kip could see his pale sad eyes, still not looking at him, never making contact. He wanted to scream at him, to demand his attention, but all he did was expel more oxygen, the last bits of the tablet turning to a paste in his mouth.

He lurched forward, feeling the oxygen evaporate.

He swam through Enos, a darker shade in the darkness. His oxygen-starved brain offered many thoughts, all presented in swirl. He could stay right here, wrapped in

Enos's skin. Maybe he would become a part of him, here in this pitch black world.

We could follow this tide to the floating library of Antilla.

Small hands pushed against Kip's back and propelled him forward. Were they approaching sunlight or was it the panicked rush of his brain, winding down? His head throbbed now as if he could feel every bit of blood pumping through it.

Even now he didn't want to leave Enos.

He heard Shadow's watery voice in his ear.

"Hold on, Kip."

Hold on.

14

Kip's hands shook, but Enos's stayed steady.

Enos worked quickly, flipping the black tie back and forth, looping and threading it, his arms around Kip.

It was Kip's Initiation Day, the time to stand in front of all his peers and be recognized.

Or be rejected.

Enos turned Kip's white pressed-collar up and then folded it back down with sharp creases.

What had they talked about?

Are you nervous?

Yes. I hate how nervous I am. I'm ready, Enos. I've prepared for this moment for five years.

That's why you're nervous. Pretend it's just a spontaneous event you're going to, unplanned.

Yes, we decided to go at the last minute. We're choosing to go.

Exactly.

And we're the youngest people there. We're the bright young things.

Of course we are.

The clock in the parlor chimed. It was time to go. They'd take a hansom to Brixton and then on to Academy Tower. They'd talk to magicians and alchemists from all over the world. Then Kip would stand in front of them all to be judged. He'd wear a mask of inoffensive politeness, trying his best to dazzle and impress. Would it be enough?

It will be enough.

Yes?

Yes, because you'll be there and I'll be there. That's enough. It's like swimming, you never forget.

But Kip hated swimming.

The water was so cold.

There was a still pool at the base of a mountain range. It was like a sheet of glass, unbroken, reflecting the sloping rocks above and the gray sky beyond. Small bubbles started roiling the surface, sending ripples across the water to lap against dark rocks.

Then an explosion of water.

Kip shot to the surface and sucked in air. It burned his lungs like fire as he tried to inhale each gulping breath, barely pausing to exhale. Shadow surfaced next to him, his body nearly invisible in the water. He circled his friend and then helped him to the water's edge.

They both rested there, their eyes dazzled by the light.

"Thank you, Shadow," Kip said, still short of breath.

Shadow responded with a firm smack on his back, helpfully trying to expel more water.

Kip pulled himself up and sat on the bank. He looked

back up at the mountain range. It plummeted down to the pool so suddenly that it looked unnatural.

They must have passed directly through the mountain. He shuddered to think of all that earth and stone above them.

Kip stood and looked for the horizon. There was a shallow stream that ran from the pool and snaked over the ground. They followed it.

The shapes of seagulls moved over head, gliding in wide circles. There was no form to them, nothing more than a shadow against a cloudy sky. Any sound they made was a distant echo.

They came over a rise, leaving the stream as it burrowed beneath a rocky hill, going where they couldn't follow.

They looked down on a flat landscape, nearly monochromatic. Kip thought he was looking at a desert, but then saw a sweep of black sand rushing towards gray water.

They had a reached an ocean, if something with no tides could be called an ocean. It was a vast plane of still water.

Kip had read that the horizon disappeared after twelve miles, but this world again defied logic. There was no drop-off to the ocean, it simply continued.

Shadow ran forward to splash in the water, his small paws leaving scattershot footprints in the sand. He bounded into the water with a dull splash then, screeching, ran back out.

"Cold!" he yelped.

Kip suddenly wanted to feel the sand between his toes. He slipped off his shoes and socks, rolled up his pants, then walked forward onto the black sand. His pale toes sank into it as a chill ran through his body.

He tied his shoes together by their laces and then slung

them over his shoulder. With one hand cupped over his brow, he searched the beach, looking for any signs of life, any clue as to where their path was leading them.

Squinting into the distance, he saw a shape through the haze. A hulking black-gray thing on the shoreline. With no other point on the horizon, they walked towards it.

As they moved closer, the black shape revealed itself in the fog. It was the remnant of a shipwreck, a mast and sail sinking below the surface. The tattered canvas waved like semaphore signals. The hull was spread wide like a broken ribcage, a hole where organs should have been. Water moved in and out of the cavern.

Kip spotted a faint hint of tracks in the sand. He followed them up the beach. They seemed tenuous, like everything else in the Pale World. Everything struggled to be real.

Two shapes huddled together on the beach. From a distance, it looked like more wreckage from the ship, washed to shore and left to rot, but as Kip and Shadow approached they could see two human forms.

Amelia Britten and Stephen Fairfield.

They were both wet. Their damp hair lay matted against their faces and their clothes clung to their bodies. A thin trickle of water continued to move over them, snaking from the tops of their heads and finding its way down to the ground where it pooled in small black puddles.

Britten sat on a gnarled piece of driftwood, looking as if she had merged with it. She was hunched over and peering down at the sand, where she traced a shape. Her finger ran in circles, forming some complex pattern over and over.

Fairfield sat on a rock with his head in his hands, gently rocking his body.

Amelia Britten looked up from her pattern in the sand.

"Master Kip, what a surprise. The strangest thing happened."

Kip stepped forward, speechless. Shadow wasn't far behind, his small arms still wrapped around his body for warmth.

"I dreamed of water," she said, looking off into the distance. "It was cold, the coldest thing I've ever felt, and it was inside me, finding its way into every part of me. And then there was nothing...nothing but stars and it was even colder still."

Fairfield spoke next.

"The gravity of the stars...we saw it pulling ... our bodies are there, even now, drifting into some uncharted place."

Kip knelt in front of Britten and took her hands. They were bitingly cold and he nearly dropped them with a gasp, but forced his fingers to hold on.

"Blackmoor did this," he said forcefully, trying to meet her eyes. She found every opportunity to look away.

"Did you ever find your lover, sweet child?" she asked, ignoring his words.

Kip let her hands fall. They went back to tracing patterns in the sand.

"No, not yet. I...I'm trying to find him."

"Was it worth it, boy?" Fairfield said from his rock, his cheeks red. "Was it worth it to abandon your duties for some romance, some cheap and tawdry thing that's as common as copulation, and just as transient?"

Kip turned on him in a rage.

"You think I wanted this? You think I asked for any of this?"

"I think you set the board, you placed the pieces. You

tantalized Blackmoor with the very thing that led us to this doom.

"And now we've been cast out into the cosmos, frozen carcasses waiting to shatter against a passing bit of debris."

He balled his fists. "I had a family, boy. Did you know that? A wife of twenty-two years, two girls. I'm sure I had two girls. I...I can't remember their names."

He trailed off, his head sinking back into his hands.

"We saw him," Britten said. "I'm sure we saw Lord Blackmoor passing by. Did he speak to us? I don't remember. He looked...old."

Fairfield coughed. "He said we sailed from Surrey, shades of ourselves."

Shadow was staring at the ship. He padded towards the shore and Kip followed.

"Does Kip see it?" his friend said.

Kip looked at the water. There was the merest hint of a path playing on the lapping waves. It moved straight towards the horizon, stretching an impossible distance towards the purple disturbance.

The place we're going, Kip thought.

The air split with the deep clang of a bell. Again, the single deafening peel that sent the Pale World into chaos. The gray sky turned black as stars stabbed down at them. Constellations rippled in the water at their feet.

Kip brought his hand to his ears, riding out the horrible sound as it faded in an echoing loop.

As quickly as it had come, it vanished. The gray board set again, waiting for the next move.

"Kip and Shadow are going to sail the sea like two privateers!" Shadow exclaimed.

He raised his hands over his head and his body went pale, all except for his eyes. The blue rolled into purple.

Still water began to churn, sea foam rising in angry circles. A swarm of purple lights became visible just below the surface like a host of jellyfish. The lights darted towards the wreckage of the ship.

It was a host of Shadows.

Kip saw one breach the water, its small black form cresting then disappearing, its body wet and slick.

These creatures were architects of this underworld, or linked to its creation somehow. The purple had returned to Shadow's eyes, only more forcefully. It slashed and cut, mixing with, and fighting, the blue.

"Shadow, be careful," Kip said, but his friend didn't seem to hear him. He didn't like him using the magic of this world, siphoning off a piece of Vorax's sorcery, if that's what he was doing.

The ship tilted to the right, showing its broken underbelly, a ragged gash in its hull, then righted itself. It was like one of the great lizards in a museum, raised from the depths. Unearthed timber and canvas revealed themselves inch by inch. The tattered sails caught the wind and billowed to life. Holes plugged, grew back together like living wood. Water flushed from every pore.

The Shadows burst out of the water and scurried over the body of the ship, mending it as they ran.

Kip and Enos sail to the Lost Library of Antilla.

This is my ship, Kip thought. Bought and paid for. If only he could sail far away and not to that purple glow on the horizon. He looked back to find Enos again as if he would offer the answers.

Enos stood a few paces back on the crest of a dune, his

feet blurring with the black sand. He was looking away from the ship at some unseen point.

Kip hated him for that. He hated him for not looking at the marvel in front of them. He hated him for his absence. He wanted to scream at him, to awake some part of him.

"We were going to sail to Antilla! This is one of your ships!" Kip yelled at his static form. "Don't you remember?"

Shame swelled in Kip. He knew Enos was dead. His love had gone before him, had suffered, and then departed, and all Kip could think about were ships in bottles and the pain that wouldn't leave his chest. He turned away from the memory.

Shadow's small body was shaking now but he kept his hold on the ship. Kip reached for him, wanting to steady him, to help him, but his hand passed through his body.

His eyes had given over to the purple light. They blazed like two beacons, a lighthouse calling the ship. It obeyed, moving clumsily in the wind as it turned and faced the shore.

"That's the ship that drowned us," Fairfield said.

"No, Stephen, it was the stars that did it," Britten corrected. "Don't you remember?"

"I'm afraid I don't, Amelia."

"I remember aperitifs and stars and coldness, and then nothing. Don't you remember the nothing?"

But Fairfield didn't respond. Instead he stepped into the water and walked towards the ship.

15

They leaned on the railing like gawking tourists, Kip, Shadow, Fairfield, and Britten all in a row. They watched the black sand and sloping cliffs of the shoreline move away from them as their ship caught the wind. The sails bellowed outward, touched by a breeze that didn't seem to effect the surface of the water. It was as still as glass.

Shadow's eyes had returned to their normal blue, but Kip wondered for how long.

"A ship needs a name," he said.

"It had a name," Fairfield said.

"No, a new name for a new world." Kip turned to Shadow. "You should name it. You resurrected it."

Shadow hung from the railing, letting his back legs dangle above the deck and looked up to the sky, deep in thought. Kip knew it wasn't something his friend would take lightly. The name would need to be perfect, not something of mere whimsy.

Amelia Britten was moving her arms over her head in

some strange pattern, doing a meditative dance, her eyes closed. Kip was reminded that the spiritualist and Fairfield were both dead. It seemed like a cloud of memory now with no clear edges. Had he really seen them cast into the stars to freeze in the depths of space?

Shadow made a sudden exclamation and jumped down to the deck.

"The Frigatebird!" he yelled.

The ship responded as if it had been waiting to be named. It lurched forward across water that was suddenly filled with chop.

"Shadow read in a book that the Frigatebird can fly over the ocean for weeks at a time. They ride the clouds. That's what we should do."

Foam-pointed waves appeared around them. The ocean had a hint of color to it, like an oil slick; many shades mixing together in a fluid dance. The sky, too, looked less cheerful now; dark enough that it blurred with the water. It made a claustrophobic dome around them. Kip felt shut in as if they were sailing in a bubble.

Or a bottle.

"I'm going to look below-deck," Fairfield said. "We'll need provisions for this trip."

Britten joined in, her voice distant.

"What provisions do you think we'll need? I can't remember wanting food or water. I can't remember what I wanted." Her voice trailed to a whisper.

"Come, Amelia. We'll look together."

As the two left, Kip looked again at the tracks of color on the water's surface.

"What do you think of the ship's new name, Enos?" Kip

asked, knowing he'd get no answer. He turned to find the shade and saw only an empty deck.

A panic seized him.

He spun around, searching. How could he have missed him?

Then he turned back to the shoreline. There, barely visible, was a dark spot. It moved like a wavering horizon on a hot day. A mirage.

The gulf of water stretched out between them, all white tips and crashing waves.

"Enos!" Kip cried. His fingers dug into the railing. He thought he would splinter it to pieces.

He called his name again and again, as if it were some spell that could summon him. But there was no magic here.

The shoreline sped away. He watched Enos flicker as he blended with the gray continent behind him, visible and then gone.

There was so much to tell him, even now. Even if he couldn't talk back, he could have listened. And yet the words weren't there. There were so many trying to get out of his head at once that it become a numb mass stuck in place.

Kip watched until the land disappeared. He watched until the gray sky deepened into dusk.

"Enos doesn't want to cross the water," Shadow said.

Kip didn't want to be on deck. The sky was too big, the water too wild.

"How can he know what he wants?" he whispered. "He's dead."

∼

Kip pushed back the door of the captain's quarters. A gust of wind rushed past him to fill the room, upsetting the layer of dust that had settled over everything. It curled into the air and was caught by the fading light that streamed through the windows.

It looked as if it had been sealed up for decades. The layer of dust formed new structures as it hid the objects it coated. It was like raiding a crypt; forgotten objects, suddenly unearthed.

Darkened iron lanterns hung from the ceiling like sleeping bats. They swung back in forth in time with the waves. There was a globe near the door. Kip ran a finger over it, lifting off the dust. The surface was blank. All lands were uncharted here.

A wooden desk stood in the center of the room, covered with objects. There were stacks of books, a quill and inkwell, a sextant, and an open ledger.

Standing over the book, Kip read the last entry:

Took on three strange passengers before leaving port. They kept to themselves but acted in the most curious manner. I greeted them briefly when they arrived, none of them carrying luggage; an older woman, a man, and a youth. What was meant as a short polite conversation, took on a different tone. They asked the same questions repeatedly, first one and then the next. I must have answered their questions about the weather a dozen times.

Regarding the weather, my first officer thinks a storm is coming. He prides himself in being able to read the clouds, an art I never mastered. Unseasonal weather surrounds the ship despite barometric readings, he says. We'll know more tomorrow with the rising sun, but for now the stars are obscured, a bad sign. I hope for smooth sailing tomorrow.

Bookmarked between two pages was a passenger manifest. Kip's finger moved down the page searching for something he didn't want to find. The last three passenger names were scribbled in messy ink.

Amelia Britten.

Stephen Fairfield.

And his own name.

Blackmoor had told the truth. This dead ship had found its way to a dead world. He shuddered to think of Britten and Fairfield in the hold right now, two shades going about their business as if nothing had happened. He thought of his own name on the manifest and wondered where his shade was. He hoped he wouldn't find out but was overcome with the feeling that some fate would draw them together again. How lonely to think of his double lost in this world.

A sharp sound broke the silence. Shadow plucked at one of the strings of a violin, a repeated E-note filled the room. It was impossible to think that this place had once known music and laughter. He could almost see it, officers sharing a drink and discussing the workings of their ship and the conditions of the sea.

Looking back to the ledger, he saw the entries start to fade. They were being reclaimed by the Pale World. All secrets needed to be kept.

Kip sat in a hard-backed chair next to the table. Using the Fixation solution, he lit a single candle. Its flame came to life, nearly buried by a rim of wax. He watched the fire spread its orange glow across the room.

A pistol next to the ledger jumped out like an exclamation point. Kip wondered if it was loaded.

Shadow approached and sat on a small stool, his paws gripping the edge of the table. He picked up the sextant and clumsily moved the pieces around, then squinted through the telescope.

Kip looked up and saw a small wooden trapdoor on the ceiling. It was open just enough to see the sky, a shifting palette of gray.

"Do you know where my shade is?"

Shadow shook his head.

"I want to say I can feel him out there, somewhere in the Pale World; that he's a part of me. But the truth is, I can't. He's as lost and mysterious as everything else in this place."

Kip was overcome with exhaustion. He leaned back in his chair and let it wash over him. As his head nodded, he felt something tug at his wrist. The metal of his bracelet caught the light as his hand fell from the arm of the chair to his lap. It was a lonely thing now, having lost its twin. Still, had he felt it move? Was something pulling it in a new direction?

A knock at the door interrupted his thoughts. Fairfield and Britten stood in the doorway. Their faces were drawn again, taken over by sorrow.

"I found something," Fairfield said, and then stepped aside.

Lord Blackmoor stood in the doorway, smiling.

16

The cabin shuddered, screaming as the wooden boards stripped back. They bent inward like curling fingers searching for a hold.

Searching for my neck.

The roof sheered away, letting in the pale light of dusk.

Lord Blackmoor directed this new destruction, his hands guiding its movement.

"A reunion of friends and colleagues," the magician said. "'Three luminaries. Three masters of intellectual thought and accomplishment in London, not to be trifled with.' I seem to remember calling you that."

Again Blackmoor had aged with some preternatural speed. His downy white hair was even thinner and now rose, untamed, from his head. His back was arched forward.

"Thank you for letting this stowaway above deck."

"I...I know you," Fairfield said. The scientist turned to face him, his eyes widening, as if seeing him for the first time.

Britten simply pointed, a witness identifying a defendant in court.

Lord Blackmoor ignored them, his eyes on Kip.

"We must talk," he said.

Long blades of stars appeared above them, like black glass catching the light. Fairfield and Britten looked up in horror. A droning sound filled the air until there was nothing else.

"No need for hangers-on," Blackmoor said over the noise.

He waved his hand and the star-scape screamed down like a hunting falcon. Britten and Fairfield blew apart like burning paper. There was no time for them to scream, no time for any reaction at all. Their ashes caught in the wind and moved upward in spirals, their remains floating through the tattered wood.

Kip watched blankly, not able to process what he'd seen. Shadow's growling brought him to his senses.

"Those two were ghosts, Kip," Blackmoor said. "Their desires are irrelevant. They're imprints left behind from a faded world. Forget them. We must talk."

Without thinking, Kip reached for the pistol on the desk. He raised it and pulled the trigger. The hammer clapped into place with a dull metallic sound. As empty and dead as the books in the room.

Blackmoor was far too amused by it. He let out a single sharp laugh as he raised his hand, closing his fist in mid-air. The pistol crumbled in Kip's hand, the metal twisting into a tortured shape. He dropped it onto the desk where it became a ball of steel.

"We must talk," Blackmoor said again. "All that matters is what we can accomplish, you and me."

Kip's mouth formed a sneer and he shouted back, naming all his grievances, wanting to hammer Blackmoor with his words, to tell him he was a liar and a murderer. But no sounds came from his mouth. He could feel his vocal cords vibrate and the air pushing from his diaphragm, but there was no sound behind it.

"It's your time to listen, boy."

Blackmoor moved his hand over his head in a slow arc and the rocking of the ship stopped. It lifted from the water like a bird taking flight. The wood creaked and moaned as it lumbered into the air. Ocean water followed it, forming constellations of droplets. The Frigatebird hung twenty feet above the water as the world froze, focused on this one moment.

"I fractured the earth under the mountain, looking for material, for some answer. But it was you who were able to mold that material into something. An alchemist can harness things that a magician cannot.

"You brought this world to life. I don't know how, I don't know what deeper magic you used, what hidden secret. But, even now, we share the same goal, finding the Soul of All Things, the tonic that creates life. It's the only way we can escape, both with our own lives, and with your beloved Enos. Why not share that burden? Why shouldn't the two great Houses of London work together once again?"

Kip looked into the stars over the magician's head, feeling their chill.

The eerie silence stretched out.

"You may speak," Blackmoor said, but it was a command not an offer.

Whatever had frozen Kip in place released him.

"It wasn't supposed to be this way!" he yelled.

And it wasn't.

"I was supposed to be in love and safe, and have adventures with someone; to see new things and feel new things. I was going to defy odds, and break rules, and be rebellious, and push outward." A vision of the well reared up in his mind, a black hole tunneling into the earth. "Not be drawn by darkness and follow it down every path. I listened to all the wrong voices, little whispering demons; stupid fucking chattering that won't leave my head. I was going to feel young. I was going to feel young forever."

Kip could have kept going. What reason was there to stop now? He could have let his tirade flow out in an endless sentence, finding every hurt and amplifying it. There was too much to say and he'd run out of words to say it. They cluttered his head, unable to come out.

Blackmoor's face was unreadable.

"Cast off this sorrow, boy! You're in the middle of a wondrous story and you're missing it. Look where we are, what we could learn!"

Kip's mind swirled. He was looking at man who had tried to kill him, a man who had killed others. A man who couldn't be trusted.

And yet.

"Why would you help me?"

Blackmoor smiled.

"I'm not helping you. I'm helping us. The Soul of All Things is the potion that will save us. Leave behind these petty grievances. You think Columbus griped when he discovered the new world? We are fashioned by adversity, sharpened to a point. That's where we realize our potential. This is greater than you and me, greater than our squabbles, greater than our houses.

"You want to defy odds, break rules, be rebellious? You want to push outward? Well, do it now, Kip. Do it now."

His mind was fractured, competing ideas threatening to pull him apart.

What if Blackmoor is right? What if it is by working together that we can find the answers?

"We're not partners. I won't trust you."

"I don't want your trust, dear boy. I want your help. And you need mine."

They left the cabin and walked onto the deck as Blackmoor lowered the ship back into the water. Kip could see the purple cloud on the horizon, still churning. The Frigatebird dipped as it caught a wave and moved forward again, finding its own course.

Behind him, the captain's quarters knitted back together, wood locking into place piece by piece like a puzzle.

Shadow was silent. He looked up at Kip, stealing glances and then looking away.

Kip wanted to explain, to soften the moment, but he couldn't think of what to say. His final objective was all that mattered. Feeling Enos's warm skin again and hearing the sound of his voice was all that mattered.

The Soul of All Things was all that mattered.

The door to the hold opened and Britten and Fairfield climbed onto the deck. Their faces were drawn and they blinked even in the fading light.

"Have...have we left Surrey?" Fairfield asked.

"We have a ship to catch," Britten added.

It was a loop. An endless loop, Kip thought.

Blackmoor laughed.

"Ah, gentle travelers, why don't you stay a while. Join me and my young companion while we talk."

The two nodded like docile animals. They were a small band of adventurers now, Blackmoor's dinner party on an expedition.

A chill fell on the ship, coming down in waves as stars appeared. Amelia Britten wrapped her arms around herself as she looked up at the sky.

"Can't we go below deck? The world is too big and cold."

They sat in a tight circle surrounded by crates and swaths of canvas. Rotting hammocks swayed back and forth. An open trapdoor above them contained the stars in a tight square.

Lord Blackmoor reached out a cupped hand and made a scooping motion. A ball of flame rolled out from his palm and hung in mid-air. It bobbed lazily, its light coloring their faces. A thin stream of smoke moved upwards and through the trapdoor.

Kip imagined the sea at night, unseen things moving in the water, driven by primitive impulses, waves tumbling in a pitch black world as the stars wheeled overhead. It felt like the ship was static as the world passed by.

He looked into one of the crates next to him, digging through chips of sawdust, hoping to find some treasure. Nestled in the bottom was a bottle filled with a cloudy white liquid. He read the label curiously.

"Coconut wine. Tagaytay, Phillipines. 1865."

The space they were in suddenly felt lived-in. *This ship has seen other shores and had other adventures. Other passengers*

have walked its deck and sat in this hold. What did they say to
each other then?*

The writing faded, leaving a blank label.

"Should we offer it to the sea as a libation?" Blackmoor
asked.

Kip thought of the last time they'd shared a drink and
the horrible turns that had unspooled from that event. He
raised the bottle and tilted it towards the fire, letting the light
illuminate it. The milky-white drink came to life, a cloudy
living gem. The cork came off with a sharp *pop*, and he raised
the bottle to his lips. The sweet liquid filled his mouth.

Kip passed the bottle, each person taking it in turn.

This is an intermission, he thought, *the held breath of the
Pale World. A ceasefire.*

He caught the way Fairfield and Britten looked at Lord
Blackmoor, their faces teetering between distrust and hatred
and then melting to a kind of forgetting.

Shadow had found a bit of canvas and made a small
divot in it. He was curled in a ball watching them, Blackmoor's fire flickering in his eyes.

They continued passing the bottle long into the night,
and with each pass there came a story.

"I'm here and I'm there," Fairfield said. "I feel the warmth
of the fire and yet part of me drifts in the cosmos, never to
come back."

Blackmoor watched him as he spoke, his expression
unreadable.

"I was once summoned by the Queen," Britten said.
"They brought me to the Blue Room of Windsor Castle, the
very room where her beloved Albert had died. They'd
already started calling her 'The Widow of Windsor' by then.

"We tried to contact Prince Albert. I promised her I could

peek behind the veil, that there would be some connection. I remember nothing from the incident, but the Queen told me I spoke with Albert's voice, I moved with Albert's movements. They say this went on for nearly six hours.

"I channeled the Prince at different ages, from childhood to his deathbed. They all converged at once. Maybe there are variants of us, all living at once, all moving through time, following our own paths."

"Victoria Rex," Fairfield said, raising the bottle.

"I hate that idea," Kip said, sullenly. "I want there to be just one me, one unique incarnation. I want all the joy and pain, tears and laughter to be mine alone."

He felt a covetous need to have it all to himself. It was unimaginable to think there were versions of him living more perfect lives. If he let his imagination wander, he could almost feel the imprint of all those Kips, as if their lives transcended universes and he was competing against each one.

What if they got to keep their Enoses?

The thought made him sick. There was a Kip waking up next to his lover, breathing in the smell of his skin, planning the day ahead, then the weeks, months, and years to follow.

"No," Blackmoor said. "If you're one of many, or rather, one of an infinite amount, than surely you're an average. Yes, some Kips may have climbed to greater heights, known more dizzying happiness, but then, by that same measure, some have known more pain, more loneliness, more sorrow. Fear not, you're merely an average."

Kip refused to believe that. His pain was too personal to be shared.

"You're Master of Alchemy House, after all. How badly could you be doing?"

He wanted to jump across the fire and slip his hands

around the magician's neck, to explain it all to him as he squeezed the life from his body. Instead, he took another swig from the bottle before passing it on.

"I believed it then and I still do," Britten said. "The dead never leave us."

Blackmoor chuckled. "Maybe they don't leave. Maybe they're doomed to live as shades, trapped in some other world. Maybe they repeat the same patterns of their death over and over again until time fades them to nothing."

The magician smiled with his mouth and nothing else. His eyes remained two stern glints.

The bottle came to Kip again and he saw that it was still full. No matter how much they drank, its contents never changed. *Maybe we'll sit here and drink forever.*

His eyes unfocused. Everything was feeling now, feeling and memory. He remembered late nights in London as alcohol amplified everything. Sights, sounds, and emotions all turned up by chemicals. It was an alchemist's dream, to give over to it.

And that's what he did.

The space between words stretched out until all conversation ended. Britten and Fairfield nodded off. Shadow was breathing heavily.

The magician studied Kip, his cold eyes catching the dim firelight that lit the hold. The shadows changed his emotions as they moved in and out of the contours of his face, now forming a smile, then a frown, then no emotion at all.

Trusting him will end in ruin, but if I get just enough of what I want...

Shadow stirred, opening one eye. He scanned the room, stopped on Kip, then went back to snoozing. Kip, too, was overcome. The bottle of coconut wine rolled gently from his hand as he leaned back on a bit of crumpled canvas, his eyes heavy.

The ball of fire bobbed as he fell asleep.

Kip woke to darkness as a voice spoke.

"Why don't we go deeper?"

He rubbed his eyes.

"Deeper?"

The silhouette of Lord Blackmoor rose, blocking the square of stars as he climbed the ladder and rose out of sight.

17

The wind was biting. It howled over the deck, its sound filling Kip's ears. The dome of stars overhead looked vast and alien.

Blackmoor stood at the prow, a darker cut in a dark sky. He spoke slowly, finding his way through some difficult thought.

"Vorax took something from me, something I can't quantify. But I also took something from him. I carry your conversations with him in my head. All those hours you spent at the well, pouring your secrets into it. I siphoned off some part of it, some essence. The memories have mixed with mine. It's an intrusion, an infiltration into my head. I thought it might drive me mad but then I chose to let it in.

"And Enos, I know him now too."

"I wish you didn't," Kip snapped. "Those are my memories."

"Oh, I didn't ask for them. My head was crowded enough already. But it's taught me one thing; this is your world. Or, at least, it's linked to your unconscious mind. You're mani-festing this."

The old man pointed to the horizon.

"And I have no doubt that whatever lies in that purple light is yours as well."

"I would never create this horrible place. I would have filled it with—"

"Your dreams?"

"Yes." *My dreams. Every inch of it would be fantasy and visions and life.*

"A world made entirely of dreams is a nightmare."

The magician reached out his hand and Kip flinched, pulling away.

"Let me show you what this world is."

He brought a finger to Kip's temple. A red ember jumped, accompanied by an electric spark. It warmed the side of his head and then sunk beneath the flesh before fading away.

"You described something to Vorax, something adrift in the ocean."

Kip felt a touch of shame as Blackmoor laid bare his thoughts.

"The Floating Library of Antilla."

"Yes, that was it."

Tears stung Kip's eyes. "It was our spot on the map, an imaginary place we were trying to get to. We made it all up."

"Let's go there now," Blackmoor said.

Kip looked out over the water. Black waves moved like streams of oil, shining under the stars.

A tower of fog rose in the distance. It moved in a clock-wise spiral, rising slowly upwards as it masked a giant shape.

The sky bent around it, making room for this new thing in the world.

Blackmoor went to the railing. He slipped over the side and into the dinghy, then gestured for Kip to do the same. Kip followed him into the boat, looking down at the black water below. The old man waved a hand at the ropes and pulleys and they moved for him, lowering the boat. The dinghy beat against the side of the ship, keeping a steady drumbeat.

They hit the water and the magician raised a single hand to take control of the boat. It matched his movements as it flowed through the water, buffeted by magic, and cut a straight line for the tower of fog.

A glow was trapped inside it, its light catching in the points of the waves and making a great blue column. Something wanted to be revealed, something wanted to struggle out of its cocoon. As the fog cleared, it revealed its secrets.

The Floating Library of Antilia.

The sight overwhelmed Kip. His imagination had always been a source of pain for him, delivering images of such beauty that he knew reality could never live up to. But this was different. It was a structure pulled from his fantasy world, fully intact, and somehow exceeding it.

The Library was made entirely of wood, richly lacquered to prevent water from destroying it. It looked untamed, not shaved down or cut so that you forgot it ever came from a tree. It could have been a Bonsai from the Orient, carefully tended. Kip imagined it being pruned and grown, taking the saltwater it needed to grow its body from the sea. *Salt – the essence of the body.*

Thin windows moved in a spiral around it, blue light glowing from each one.

It is too fanciful, Kip thought. *Even for me.*

As they drew closer something knocked the side of the boat, at first a gentle nudge then a more forceful push.

"What is it, Kip?" Blackmoor whispered.

Kip ignored Blackmoor as his fear grew. *How much of my fantasy has been brought to life? How much of my fantasy can we survive?*

A shape broke the surface, black and oily with pinpricks of glowing light along its surface. It appeared on their right side and then their left. It moved warily, testing this new thing in its grasp.

"Enos and I imagined a guardian for the library, something to protect all this knowledge."

"What did you imagine?"

"We...we called it the Dark Leviathan of Antilia."

"Of course you did," the magician sighed. "And, in these imaginings, how did you defeat it?"

"We didn't. We skipped over that part."

"That doesn't surprise me, either." Blackmoor brought his fists together and closed his eyes. There was a crackling sound as if something were tearing at the space between his fists, then a burst of hot blue light. It moved like lightning over his flesh, flaring and then retreating again and again.

He raised his hands in the air, casting the light over the water. The dark shapes retreated, churning in the water as they dove out of sight.

A moment passed before they came back, now more curious.

Black tentacles latched onto the stern of the boat. One slid over Kip's hand. He heard the wood creak under their grip. Water flooded the bottom of the boat, running through cracks in the wood.

The ocean boiled as a rounded head emerged from the darkness. A row of eyes blinked to life. They were eight black marbles hidden behind blinking gray membranes. The eyes dilated as they took in the curious new thing they'd found.

Then it opened its mouth.

It was something born from a nightmare, all its pointy edges intact.

A horrible shrieking came from the open mouth, sending waves up through its flesh. It entranced Kip, like looking into some unending depth. Deeper and deeper it went, past circular rows of teeth. Some inner light glowed through the flesh, moving out of the mouth and then speeding over the body, past black eyes and over gray skin.

The ship jolted as more tentacles found the boat, locking to its sides with a suctioned grip. The thing lifted them out of the water and tilted the boat towards its mouth.

The mouth spoke to Kip.

Come closer, it said. *Come closer and stay for a while. There are no problems past these teeth. A mere prick and then blackness; stillness.*

The call of the creature filled one ear, while a screaming voice filled the other.

Lord Blackmoor.

"Get down, Kip!" his voice echoed.

A blast of lightning sped over Kip's head, making his hair stand on end. It shot into the beast's mouth. Its eyes widened as it took in the energy. Horrible choking sounds rose up through its gullet, as if the creature were torn between gorging itself or escaping.

It dove beneath the water to avoid the lightning blast. Its tentacles let go of their hold on the boat. Kip looked over the side to see a thousand glowing spots moving in the water and then spiral out of sight.

Blackmoor busied himself with some new spell. He bowed his head as the red light burned beneath his eyelids. He grabbed the sides of the boat, his hands looking skeletal and weak. The boat reacted to his touch. It lurched forward and then sped across the water, kicking up sea foam.

The creature followed their wake. The water swelled to a mound as its massive form broke the surface. Its tentacles pushed it in the water like a great serpent. It's horrible mouth gaped wide open.

The Library's tower swayed overhead as they sped closer. Kip spied an intricate wooden staircase at its base. The tangle of stairs led to a massive wooden door that had a single brass horn in the center of it, in place of a doorknob.

Blackmoor didn't slow down. Their boat crashed into the stairs, splinters of wood filling the air. Kip was thrown forward, off the boat, and onto the pier. He flew across its slick surface and crashed into the bottom stair.

There was a roar behind them as the beast came on, the distance between them much too small.

Its eyes blazed. An angry scorch mark cut across its skin, deadening two of its eyes and ripping the corner of its mouth. The shriek rattled in Kip's chest.

Kip scrambled up the stairs as Blackmoor followed.

The magician moved his hands in a circle, forming a shield made of light. It looked like a glass lens filing the air, catching the starlight above. Its edges burned the wood that surrounded them.

The creature mounted the stairs and threw its weight against the shield, pushing Blackmoor back against the door and taking Kip with him, only the magic of the shield protecting them. The beast snapped at them, black salvia spattering the wall of magic between them.

"How do you open the door?" Blackmoor yelled.

The answer was another bit of fantasy. There was some half-baked idea in Kip's mind, a detail he and Enos never fleshed out..

Another stupid romantic notion, he thought.

He leaned forward until his mouth was cupped by the brass horn on the door, and whispered a single word.

"Chickadee."

It was the bird that Enos had picked in the marketplace. The chickadee, a symbol of 'clarity and purity of soul.' Where was it now? Still flying over rooftops?

A vibration moved through the metal. A massive bolt slid out of place and the two doors opened inward.

Blackmoor pushed his arms out and the glowing shield moved away. It flew outward, smashing into the creature's face, knocking teeth from its jaws. They fell into the dark water like small stones. Its tentacles tried to grab the edge of the shield and were sliced open. It screamed again as black liquid spilled from its flesh and boiled in the water.

Kip and Blackmoor ran through the doors, leaving the horror behind. The heavy wood slammed shut, cutting off all sound and throwing them into darkness.

18

"What a creative mind you have, Master Kip," the magician said in the darkness. "Let's see what it's really made of."

A blue light filled the tower. It moved down from a great height, lighting the interior as it came. Wooden columns as thick as trees held the structure up, each one supporting a balcony. There were carvings in the wood written in a secret language. They made a web of symbols and words, one running into the next like a run-on sentence. Each balcony had a ladder and a row of bookshelves.

And the books.

In his lifetime Kip had spent hours cradling books, his fingers moving over the spine and the embossed print that told him what adventure awaited. He'd open the book gently, stretching the spine in fifty-page increments to break it in. He'd note the typeface and kerning and then put his face between the pages, taking in the smell of the pulp.

It would take him a thousand lifetimes to perform that ritual here.

Books filled every space. The blue light revealed them, floor by floor, until it reached the base of the tower. The floor was made of intricate circles of wood, different shades and finishes that formed the shape of a compass. Replacing North, South, East, and West, were unknown characters that looked almost musical. This might have been one of the poles of the world, everything else attracted to it.

The blue light of the tower illuminated the floor and the one thing that filled the space, a reading table and a single chair. All the information in the world offered to one person at a time.

The table was crowded with small towers of books, spines cracked and worn, pages yellowed. As Kip approached he saw a form filling the chair.

It was the shade of Enos.

His body was as grey and transparent as ever but his mood had changed. Gone was the passive lost Enos. He was smiling with some delight, one coming after the next, as he looked down at an open book on the table.

He turned his head and spoke, wordlessly, to someone out of sight.

He's talking to me, Kip thought. *I should be here with him, exploring every wonder in this tower. In some alternate universe, I'm there, right at his side.*

He could almost see himself climbing the ladders, blowing dust off one new treasure after the next, stopping to discuss his findings with Enos. All the knowledge in the world passing into his mind, filling every corner of his brain like water filling a bottle.

Blackmoor spoke. "Come back, Kip. Come back and let's finish what you started."

Kip forced himself to look away from the table.

"What's the second element?" the magician asked.

"Salt."

Lord Blackmoor nodded and then closed his eyes. The ember-light returned, glowing through the flesh of his eyelids. His stretched his arms towards the floor, his hands locked in two fists.

There was a pause and Kip could feel energy gathering.

Blackmoor opened his fists and two streams of fire punched from his open hands. The floor lit up with an explosion of color then warped and cracked as the wooden boards peeled back like the petals of a flower opening.

Enos continued his reading, unaware of the blaze of light that cut through the floor mere feet from the reading table.

The circle deepened until it hit seawater. A spray of foam shot into the air angrily. A vortex of water spun wildly below them as a light grew from its center.

He looked down into the inner chambers of the Pale World, and perhaps beyond. Was this the material that held the world together, that held the universe together?

Colors swirled in the depths, colliding with one another as sparks of light shot through the column of water.

"Why did you bring me here?" Kip said.

"You brought us here," Blackmoor said. "Should we go deeper? Let me help you along. Let's see what we can uncover."

The magician reached out again and touched his temple. There was an electric spark as a red ember jumped.

"Recall your Initiation Day."

"Why?"

"Let's see what will happen."

Kip looked down into the glowing whirlpool and then closed his eyes. He focused on that moment in time, fighting back the forgetfulness of the Pale World and felt a pain in his head as he did. It moved in like a blade severing gray matter then slowly eased as visions came.

"Now open your eyes."

Kip opened one eye slowly, as if he were peeking at something he shouldn't have been.

Reality had blended with memory.

The hole in the floor was still there, water churning in an angry circle, but it was anchored to the floor of a great hall. He was in the interior of the Academy Tower. A massive structure of white granite that looked like ivory or bleached bone, a pristine and mysterious place.

Kip stood in the center of the floor. A circle of stairs surrounded him, making an amphitheater. The white marble under his feet was cut with thin ebony in a kaleidoscopic pattern.

The center of the tower was carved out, a giant column of open air that stretched to the top of the structure. Many rooms and chambers were built around it, each under an arched doorframe. They filled every floor.

A green light shone at the very top. It pulsed and moved slowly in the shadows above.

But here on the ground was the moment Kip had summoned.

His Initiation Day.

It was the moment he'd graduated from his apprenticeship to that of a full alchemist.

Robed figures filled the stairs around him, each watching with stoic duty. Kip had never been so intimidated, so sure that he would make a fool of himself. Had he tricked them all to reach this position? What kind of imposter was he?

"Unacceptable!"

A voice cut through the staid atmosphere. An old man rose weakly from his seat, using a cane as a prop.

"I didn't give my life in service of the Great Houses of London to see a homosexual take up the mantle."

There was a quick eruption in the hall, many voices shouting over one another.

Kip had hoped most would be coming to his defense, but the tangle of shouts seemed too aggressive, too rehearsed for that. He knew in that moment how much they hated him, how much they would do to stop him. His nerves collapsed. He was just a kid again, a kid who knew nothing, who didn't belong.

Who was undeserving.

"Moral deviancy!" someone shouted.

"The corruption of a Great House!"

The first man who had spoken took off a shoe and threw it across the audience. It hit one of Kip's few defenders square in the face.

They were actually fighting in the great hall of Academy Tower.

Every bit of anxiety bared down on him, ready to rob him of his voice, his nerves, every inch of himself. Then he saw a face in the crowd.

Enos.

He didn't do much, just the slightest gesture, a single confident nod. It was enough. The claws that gripped him loosened, bit by bit, until he felt his chest rising as he took in air.

Lord Blackmoor was at his side.

"Look where you've brought us, Master Kip."

"I didn't. It's a trick of the Pale World."

Blackmoor tilted his head as if considering this.

"Who's to say? You know tricks better than mine. Yet, it proves my thesis, Kip. Only magic matters in the coming century. Look at where we are, what you can manifest. Give up your tinkering and join me. Look what we could achieve."

"I don't know if this is magic."

"What else could it be?"

Kip didn't know but it unsettled his mind. He looked at the faces sneering at him. Their shouts were muted now, turned down to a background whisper.

All strangers but for those green eyes.

"How do I stop it?"

"Make an offering. What do you have to offer?"

Kip knew immediately. He had one relic left in his reliquary, Enos's hair. He pulled it from his bag now, a tight bundle of black tied with a red string. It moved over his fingers, still so soft and alive. He brought it to his face and inhaled, smelling it for the last time.

Maybe this was another kind of initiation.

Kneeling, he took out the necessary tools from his bag. The copper plate, two drams of borax and one of antimony. He cupped the bundle of hair over the plate. His hands shook.

How can I let this go?

His mind pleaded with him. It tried to find another plan, anything to keep Enos in his clutches, even if it were something so small and dead.

I'll never let go.

He let go.

The hair fell to the plate and disappeared into a green

fire. An acrid smell filled his nose as smoke danced off the plate, obscuring the process.

He tilted the plate and knocked the contents into the whirlpool below. It took them greedily, ready to consume his offering. The column of water shifted between every shade of blue, pulsing in a quick cycle. Streams of water grabbed the mixture as the smell of burnt hair rose from the whirlpool.

When the water retreated, a single sphere of blue light remained.

Kip took the vial containing the essence of mercury from his pocket and held it out, the orange light whirling behind the glass. The two energies attracted one another like two poles of a magnet.

The blue orb danced to meet its counterpart, swirling around the lip of the glass before slipping into the vial. He corked it carefully and watched the two merge. It flared in his hand, again sending out its warmth.

Academy Tower faded as the overlay of the library returned. White marble turned into wood, purple light turned to blue. Kip was happy to escape the eyes of the crowd, to be free of their judgement. This was a safer place. Let him stay buried among these books.

"We manifest our world," Blackmoor said. "Didn't you say that at the dinner party? Shared subjective reality powers the world. This one is no different, it's just more literal. A dream in our world must be coaxed to life with attention and work. It must be attended to for years so that it can grow.

"Here you can manifest your dreams and nightmares.

You can bring this to life." He gestured to the library above them. "Maybe the Pale World is the raw material Vorax said it was."

Blackmoor returned his gaze to Kip. "Build the world you want to see. And when you've built it all, Kip, there's only one thing left to create."

Blackmoor's eyes were sharp diamonds catching the light from the whirlpool. A smile spread across his face as he spoke two words.

"Dark House."

Dark.

House.

Some lumbering thing shifted in Kip's head. It was all black, a shadow that had hidden deep within his mind without detection. Memories he had never made came into focus, a stream of images.

A structure made of stars and the empty space between them. The heavens bent to form walls and vaulted ceilings. It was expansive but also contained.

The heart of it was a pure black, darker than any shade.

Kip went blind to everything else but the vision. He stumbled forward, grabbing the folds of Blackmoor's jacket.

"Dark House," he whispered.

"Yes," Blackmoor said. "The place I'm trying to get to. Make it real, Kip. It's hidden in our world, but you can make it real again.

"It's where you got your power. Your sorrow brought it forth. You found your twin in that power, darkness finding darkness."

Kip knew he was right. Enos's death had torn a hole in his brain. Some thought had burrowed deep into his mind, like a maggot into soft meat. It found some depth where it could hide and grow and all manner of things had come from it.

The well that broke from the earth.

The dark tree limbs growing through Alchemy House.

A Shadow found him.

An underworld created from sorrow.

"Let it grow now, Kip, unrestrained."

"What have you done, Blackmoor?"

"Only what was necessary. Magic and alchemy joined together in the end. You just needed my help. I put the trigger in your mind and you pulled it."

Then came the bell; another deafening tolling. Kip looked up to see the night sky through the top of the tower. Crystal starlight whirled above. In another life, the smog of London choked out the stars and made one forget their place in the world. It was a dangerous thing to forget.

The vision hurried on. It was a feral animal unleashed in his mind. The floor heaved, answering the vision. Kip could feel every wave that rocked the tower, every beast that moved beneath the water, all of it flowing to one place:

Dark House.

"Rushing to the end," a voice spoke.

Kip turned to the chair. Enos was gone, replaced by a black cloud. It came together layer by layer as it found its shape. Blue-orb eyes appeared in the deep back of the chair and moved forward as they settled into place.

Vorax smiled.

"What a pleasure to watch you. Are all humans filled with such doubts, such anxieties? Do you all cloud your purpose like this? Zigzagging when you should be moving in a straight line?"

Kip pushed away from Blackmoor, hating the feel of his

touch, the texture of his clothing. He swooned, nearly falling to the floor, the visions still streaming into his head. Each layer was darker than the next. He was traveling through the cosmos slowly leaving each star behind, each source of light lost to blackness.

"Do you know I can see your heart beating? Yours is so healthy and vital. The old man's weakens. I can see the straining of the tissue, the wearing down of the parts, all the little cracks that will speed his end."

Blackmoor sneered.

"You have no right!"

Vorax turned to face him, his eyes moving like searchlights.

"You went looking, old man. You can't complain when you catch a tiger on a tiger hunt. You wanted a peak behind the veil. You wanted power." He pointed at Kip. "You tangled yourself with this human, this strange human who bent the world with his grief."

He smiled again, sharp black teeth flashing.

"Do you think Dark House will provide the answers? Meet me there, magician, if you can."

His body burst into a thousand pieces. Streaming blackness rose from the chair, spinning like a tornado, Kip and Blackmoor at the center of it. Books and papers caught in the wind as it moved upward. The blackness sped towards the hole at the top of the tower, obscuring the stars.

Vorax's laughter was everywhere.

"Bring your potion to me, human boy. Bring your potion across the sea."

The sneer was still on Blackmoor's face as he turned to Kip.

"Time to end this absurd errand. Take your fucking Soul

of All Things and choke on it. It's the pursuit of a fantasist, a child. Dark House is the real seat of power, and to Dark House we will go."

The sound of rushing water filled Kip's ears.

The tower rocked back and forth, a buoy on the open sea. The churning of the waves reached a thunderous pitch and then something struck the side of the tower. The wall of the library turned to a twisted wreck, books exploded outward, followed by shards of wood and a flood of seawater.

Blackmoor had called The Frigatebird.

The prow pierced the wall like a harpoon finding the soft spot of its target. It was a deadly hit, sending shudders up the interior of the tower. Dust fell from above, mixing with stray papers that danced in the air.

The floor heaved and buckled as Kip lost his balance, nearly toppling into the chasm in the floor. He hit the table instead. It slid back, slamming into the chair where Vorax had been and cracking it in half.

The mast of the ship appeared, breaking through the weakened structure. Its sails torn to shreds, they flapped like broken wings.

All the while, Dark House danced in Kip's head. Arches, doorways, towers, windows. All were black and alien. And the stars, so many stars, were woven into its structure. How could something be so clear and yet so unfocused? Fully understood and yet incomprehensible?

"Our ship awaits, Master Kip," Blackmoor laughed as paper and dust swirled around him. He gestured to the crumbling walls of the tower. "All these books, all these stories, speed towards a climax. This is ours!"

19

T he ship cut through floorboards, speeding towards Kip and Blackmoor. It lowered itself until the deck was at their feet, the water churning around them. The magician grabbed Kip and dragged him onboard.

Water flooded the deck, loose pages and water-logged books following the current.

Blackmoor raised his arms and the ship responded. It ground through the floor of the library and then pierced the opposite wall, punching out wooden beams and bookcases until the open ocean was visible beyond. The ship birthed itself from the tower, leaving a broken husk behind.

The shadow of Vorax still streamed from the top of library, flooding a now gray sky like chimney smoke. Dawn was coming. Thousands of eyes appeared in the cloud as it spread. Pairs of purple lights became Shadows of their own, until an army of them moved overhead, Vorax leading them.

The top of the library bent and then rolled to one side, before shearing away. It collapsed, ripping a long hole into the side of the tower as it fell. Books flowed from the wound, fluttering like baby birds leaving the nest.

Kip screamed as he clutched his head. Something so beautiful shouldn't be destroyed. All its knowledge, all its secrets, bled into the ocean and sank beneath the waves.

The light from the whirlpool broke through the crumbling tower. It shot out of each new hole like a broken lighthouse before the entire structure collapsed in an explosion of water.

Drops of rain spattered the deck.

Kip righted himself as the vision of Dark House became a reality. It no longer bewildered his mind. It felt real. Complete. He knew it waited for him somewhere over the ocean.

He got to his feet, clutching his green bag.

The door to the hold burst open, splinters of wood spinning across the deck, as Shadow, Britten, and Fairfield broke out. Shadow rushed to Kip's side.

"He made us sleep, Kip. Shadow didn't want to sleep."

Blackmoor laughed as he faced them all.

"What a glorious reunion this is! Two ghosts, an upjumped animal, and a boy. As I told you in Magic House, none of you has the vision for the times to come." He looked out over the gray sea and to the purple haze on the horizon. "All our answers lie there."

Amelia Britten followed his gaze as if seeing the purple light for the first time.

"No!" Britten exclaimed. "We can't go back there. That horrible purple place. That's where it begins and ends."

Fairfield was in agreement. He raced to the wheel and spun it towards the port side, causing the ship to lurch and stutter in the water. They were nearly thrown off balance as the rudder fought the sudden change of direction. The sails clapped in the wind above.

In a flash of crimson light, Fairfield was thrown over the wheel and against the railing at the fore of the ship. His back punched a hole in the wooden bannister and he crumpled forward, hitting the deck.

Lord Blackmoor radiated energy as he stood against them, his eyes two red blades again.

"We're going to the purple fucking horizon," he barked. "Before it's too late."

Even with this show of power, he looked more worn than he had hours before. His skin was like tissue paper moving over bones. Kip imagined it was something you'd see on an exhumed corpse, a silent howl on its face.

"Don't you fools feel it? Time is speeding by, robbing me of the little I have left. You may want to be errand-boys for Vorax, but I intend to solve the deeper mysteries of this place."

The ship continued to steer off its course and it angered the sea around them. White caps pricked the surface like small teeth.

Blackmoor raised his hands to the gray sky above and tried to bring forth the stars, the same cold void that had consumed Britten and Fairfield.

The spiritualist looked up in horror like a panicked animal. She was waiting for the black curtain to fall. The star-scape stuttered overhead, moving in and out of focus.

Kip could feel the chill shedding from it, buffeting the ship with frozen air.

He can't do it, he thought, *he's losing his powers*. Kip's hands roamed frantically through his bag, searching for something he could weaponize.

Decomposition.

I can help the old man along, help him meet the death he fears so much.

The stars above faltered for one last time, then disappeared with a rending *crack*. They left behind an agitated sky that swirled with thick black clouds. The world above was one giant storm system, rotating in a lazy circle.

The ship was a few hundred feet off its path, coasting into uncharted water. The white caps turned to waves that slammed against the side of the ship; the deck jelly under their feet.

Lord Blackmoor seemed confused by his lack of power. He stared at the sky in bewilderment, his hands still raised; white palms against black clouds.

Kip pushed Shadow behind him and then stepped forward.

He had something in his hand, wrapped in a white cloth. Leaning forward, he flung it at Blackmoor's feet. Tiny black spheres bounced across the deck, weaving patterns on the wood, before settling beneath the magician.

The coal-like material shattered into a fine dust and swept around Blackmoor, wrapping him in its folds. He made a sound like he'd been struck and his eyes met Kip's. Was there a look of betrayal there, even after all they'd been through? It vanished in a flash as the red returned, more violent than before. His eyelids closed, the amber light shining through the flesh.

The Decomposition material ate at the deck, dissolving wood and nails and leaving carbon behind. The smoke enveloped Blackmoor, an angry curtain of dust.

His voice stabbed out from behind its folds.

"You think you can hurt me?"

A red flare pierced the smoke and was met with a gust of wind coming off the ocean. It howled over the water, across the deck, and rushed over Lord Blackmoor. It swept the Decomposition material away, excavating Blackmoor like a fossil from the ground.

A red energy moved over his body, in constant battle with the effects of Kip's alchemy. The potion ate away his skin, a creeping black moved up his arms. It looked like he was wearing black gloves, tattered fabric weaving around his flesh. The blackness blistered and popped, creating fissures in his skin, only to be beaten back by his magic, his pale flesh knitting together again.

Slowly he fought off the Decomposition until his body returned to normal.

He stepped out of the scorched circle on the deck and towards Kip, the weary smile back on his face.

"Did I not tell you that Magic is the supreme force in the world, in this one or any?"

He cast his arm toward the captain's wheel and tried to correct its course. The wheel stuttered and made a cracking sound before falling apart. The mechanism had broken.

Vorax's black veil swept overhead, carrying its long train behind. The purple orb-eyes of a thousand Shadows played in its wake, trailing like a meteor shower, some massive heavenly body broken into a thousand pieces.

A hurricane followed them, stabs of lightning at its center. It boiled with anger, sucking up ocean water in great columns and thundering it back to the surface where it pelted the ocean with a thousand knives.

Britten helped a limping Fairfield across the deck and towards the safety of the cabin below. Again, they didn't seem real to Kip. They truly were two shades, acting out some preordained drama.

Vorax's laughter echoed down on them, coming in waves like the tide. His eyes gleamed at the head of the black veil, his sweeping robes fading to the horizon.

Blackmoor looked up.

"He doesn't want us leaving the path. He's not done with his games. I don't think I'll wait for the storm, Master Kip. But I think you deserve better company in my absence."

The magician looked from the host of Shadows above and then back to Kip's singular friend.

"Let's give your friend a little nudge," he laughed. "Let's reveal his true nature."

A purple dagger shot from his extended finger and struck Shadow in the chest. Kip's friend tumbled backwards, his form wavering.

Kip jumped forward to grab Blackmoor. He wanted to hurt him, to wound him in some way, physical pain being only the first step. But the old man had begun to fade, his body flickering like a dying candle.

Kip lost his hold on Blackmoor; his hands snapped on thin air as he tried to grab him. He imagined his hands around the magician's pale throat; imagined squeezing until all life ended.

Blackmoor moved backwards through the railing and out over the open sea. All Kip could see were his two red eyes speeding across the water.

"Goodbye for the present," his voice called, nearly lost in the storm. "Thank you for bringing Dark House to me."

Cursing, Kip looked back to Shadow. His back was turned to him; hunched over, one paw resting on the deck.

His form was agitated; tiny ripples floated off its surface and evaporated into the air.

"Shadow?" Kip took a step forward and Shadow turned to face him.

His eyes were purple, a ghastly vivid color that had beaten back the soft blue. Small drops of blue light remained in the center of each pupil, but they were contracting, disappearing to nothing.

"Kip," Shadow said, his child-echo voice filled with pain. "I'm sorry, Kip. Shadow fought it as long as he could."

"No! There's something I can do. There has to be something. Hold on, my friend." Kip reached for his bag, his fingers outstretched, as something hit the ship. The first wave of the storm was on them, accompanied by the wall of Shadows.

The deck heaved sickly, slamming them both to the port side. The ship's railing cracked Kip in the ribs, pushing the air out of him. Shadow moved more fluidly. A piece of him punched out, scurried up the railing, and clawed at Kip's hand, drawing thin slivers of blood.

Kip gasped and brought his hand to his chest. He stared into his friend's eyes, eyes that had now surrendered to purple.

"I can help you!" Kip yelled as the squall hit them. A million cold knives of rain cut him, battering his face and drowning his voice.

I'm sorry.

Kip heard the voice in his head as Shadow lunged forward. The Shadow army in the air followed his lead, descending on the ship. Blurred purple light cut through the storm, moving in wide arcs before attacking. A wave of Shadows sped toward the sails and shredded them. They came apart like ruined and tattered flesh, the ghostly fabric was caught by the storm and moved in a whirlwind around the ship.

And Vorax laughed. He spiraled above the ship, above the storm, to watch his handiwork. The hurricane had caught them and sent its lightning down in fierce blasts, illuminating the world with blinding light. In-between the blasts Kip saw his friend turned to a fierce beast. Shadow lunged forward.

His body covered Kip's with a suffocating closeness, his spectral-shape always so curious, was now a threat, a weapon. The darkness swelled around him and lifted him into the air. Kip reached out a desperate hand and grabbed the loop of his bag a split second before it was out of reach.

Lifted over Shadow's head, he looked down into the blaze of purple. It was tipping to a hot white, his power amplified by the storm. It swelled in the darkness; cut down by each lightning strike, only to come back stronger.

Kip's mind had no time to catch up, no time to process. He was suddenly airborne, tossed by Shadow, lifted by the storm, and thrown nearly the length of the ship. He hit the deck, now slick with rain, and slid the rest of the way before hitting the stern. The splintered boards grabbed at his clothes and cut any bare skin.

Shadow ran towards him, darting from one dark contour to the next as he came.

Tears and diluted blood ran down Kip's face. His voice was lost in the storm but he screamed anyway, screamed to his friend and to the world and to things beyond. He reached into his bag mindlessly. There was no time to think, no time to be clever, only to react.

His hand slipped inside a leather pouch and the powder

inside. He grabbed a handful and threw it into the air in front of him. It flowed out in spidery lines, dancing in the wind, caught in the tight columns of air that battered the ship.

The substance hit the sheets of water that thundered against the deck and turned them to a solid mass. They froze into heavy stalagmite shapes, making thick bars between him and Shadow.

Congelation crystalizes a liquid into a solid.

Shadow clawed at Kip's new cage, his purple eyes glowing through the solidified water.

"I'm sorry!" Kip yelled. It was all he could think to say.

I brought us here. I fashioned the world to be this way.

The ship rocked again, this time tipping towards the starboard side as the wind hammered it. The port side cracked under the pressure of the storm and Kip heard the rending sound of splintering wood, like the breaking bones of a giant. The railing gave way and hung uselessly like a broken arm.

Vorax and the Shadows lingered overhead, circling in the eye of the storm. Kip thought he could hear laughter piercing the tempest, dancing between thunderclaps. He thought he could hear Vorax mocking, always mocking. He wanted Kip back on the path, but he wanted to cause pain in the process, to use those around him and then cast them away.

The structure formed by the Congelation still grew, spreading its branches upward like a tree made of ice. Its weight dragged down the back of the ship, sending frigid water onto the deck.

With each lightning strike, the structure blazed to life like a prism overloaded by light. Shadow disappeared with each blaze, then came back more strongly, his claws tunneling through the ice. He was making sounds that Kip had never heard before, animal sounds that were painful to hear.

The wolf at the zoo reared up in his mind again; the void of its eyes, the pain in its voice.

The stern of the ship dipped fully into the water just as lightning struck the Congelation tower. It shattered like crystal and then collapsed, shearing off like a falling ice shelf and burying Kip and Shadow in its debris. Thousands of ice slivers hit Kip, some bludgeoning, some cutting, each more painful than the next. Shadow, too, squealed as they pelted his body. Even still, he tried to reach Kip, his small arm outstretched and his teeth gnashing.

And his purple eyes.

A wave came from the right and hit Kip with a blast of briny water. It took the jigsaw pieces of ice with it, and pulled Kip's bag from his hand.

He reached for it too late, his fingers grasping the rough wood of the deck. The wave sent the bag over the edge and into dark water.

The bag was his only weapon, and it was gone. What was an Alchemist without his tools? A writer without a pen?

A weight landed on Kip's chest, punching the air from his lungs. He thought of a demon settling on a sleeping man's chest, extracting every ounce of breath. Shadow grabbed Kip's collar and pulled him up to a sitting position, his burning eyes filling Kip's vision. The creature that had been his friend opened its mouth, showing his blunt but deadly teeth, and the depths of his gorge.

He's going to bite my head off, Kip thought wildly. He wanted to laugh at the thought, laugh and never stop;

laughing as Shadow digested him. Blackmoor had unleashed something in him that couldn't be stopped.

"I'm sorry," he said again as he brought his hands up, trying to push back against Shadow's form. Feeling his strange skin for maybe the last time.

Shadow's mouth widened.

The deafening peal of the bell struck the air, another gong marking his time here, cataloging each broken piece of it. The world froze. Kip again heard a voice as the rolling clang of the bell vanished.

Kip, is that you? I'm here! I never left!

Then it faded as quickly as it had come.

The bell changed the movement of the Shadows above. They coalesced around Vorax, drawn to his power, finding the folds of his cloak like children clutching for their mother.

His Shadow stopped too, commanded by something unheard. He craned his neck to look up at the storm, searching the sky for some new command. His hands released Kip and he fell back onto the deck. Shadow looked down at him for a moment, his purple eyes blank and lifeless, then leapt into the air.

He moved over the ship in a wide arc then rose upward until he joined with the rest of his kind, lost in a sea of black and purple.

Vorax's floating shape sprung to life and sped away from Kip and the boat, dragging his long train behind.

Kip crawled forward on the deck.

"Shadow! Don't you leave me, too!" he screamed. "Don't leave me all alone!"

But they were gone, retreating to the purple cloud far off on the horizon. Kip made it to the prow, his fingernails digging into hard wood. He pulled himself up to face the storm. He wanted to scream again, but bared his teeth instead, like a feral animal withstanding pain.

I will lash myself to this prow, Kip thought. *I will withstand whatever comes.*

The storm strengthened. Its only purpose was to destroy. It hit the ship and cracked it in half. One mast went down like a felled tree, sheared in the middle. As it sped towards the deck, Kip wondered if he could count its rings. How many years had that mast stood, what would be the final count that marked its end?

He was thrown into the air as ocean water slammed his face. As he tumbled, he saw the sky and the water flipping past, one replaced by the other with terrible speed.

I'm flying, he thought.

The last thing he remembered was the purple glow in the distance.

It was calling him, always.

20

Kip and Enos took a hansom back from Academy Tower, staring out the window at the darkening city. The last sliver of sunlight made a world of orange and blue, cobblestones and rooftops. The trotting horse kept time with heavy footfalls.

Kip was the master of Alchemy House now.

The rabble had had their say. They'd screamed and yelled. They'd called him names. But in the end, he was accepted into the order.

Kip's fingers were linked with Enos's across the cushion of the hansom. He turned to him.

What had he said?

They hate me. So many of them hate me. The way they sneered at me...

It has nothing to do with you.

But, it must.

No, they just hate an idea in their head, an ignorant stupid idea. You'll prove them wrong. The old and ignorant die and make way for the new. You'll be so good they can't ignore you.

Kip wasn't sure. Why did he have to be better just to win acceptance? Couldn't he just be like everyone else? He changed the subject.

What do we do now?

Bonfire Night is this Friday. We can go out. We can celebrate. You need some fireworks immediately!

I think you're right. Just promise me they'll have every color.

I promise.

It was enough. He would be with Enos. He'd passed his test. He'd graduated.

He'd survived the storm.

The light approached again, golden white and buzzing with some intangible energy. The sound of a chorus came with it, many voices singing in perfect unison.

Kip dreamed of breaking clouds, splintered by golden light. It pierced cumulus and cumulonimbus, and stretched to the heavens. The voices seemed to drive the light on as they smashed through a gray world, finding every spot that had been robbed of color and breathing new life into it.

The sound rose and fell, rose and fell, like waves crashing on a shore.

The voices turned to sea foam.

It muttered with its constant motion, moving in and out.

He was doused with it, bitingly cold and salty.

The dream of light faded and Kip shuddered back to consciousness. He sucked air into his lungs, each breath filling them with cold blades.

Kip pushed his body off the sand, balanced on his hands

and knees, wanting to collapse back into the water, wanting to let it drag him back out to sea. It seemed like a place where he could forget, wrapped in seaweed, coral sprouting from his skin; a place to spend the eons.

Water flowed from his hair and off his clothing, like liquid squeezed from a sponge. It was sucked back into the sand where tiny bubbles rose to the surface.

Morning had come. The storm had broken on the shore and was replaced with sunlight. Its light played off the sand, making a million small jewels.

Kip dared to look back at the sea. It moved with no memory of what had come before; no memory of ship-wrecks and lost friends.

Shadow was lost, his only and dearest friend.

His bag, that reliquary of alchemy, had sunken to the depths.

Even Fairfield and Britten were gone.

And Enos.

Kip felt a warmth spreading from his forehead and he brought his hand up to find blood there. It coated his fingers like a red glove and he watched it cover his fingerprints before dripping into the sand.

There was a beat in his breast pocket; a small thumping vibration.

He pulled out the vial, its churning light bringing color back into the world. It was a tiny engine of warmth. He hadn't lost everything after all.

The light hugged the wall of glass, pushing towards his bloody fingers, hitting the glass barrier again and again.

Does it want my blood?

Mercury, Salt...

And Sulfur.

Sulfur was abundant in the body. It turned to red liquid when burned. It was brimstone, linked to fire for as long as there had been anyone to link it. It was in the blood.

Kip realized the Pale World didn't need symbology. It didn't need tinctures and potions and chemical recipes, it was a living laboratory. Its structure had always been fluid, right from the start, as if it could change at any moment; sprouting a mountain here, collapsing a tunnel there, making a library, making a ship.

Blood pays for the passage.

He uncorked the vial and brought his bloody fingers to the glass lip of the tube. It excited the substance that lived there and it swam up to meet him. The blood was drawn into the light in thin streams and then spun like thread until it disappeared. The bauble of light turned red and then settled back into the vial.

What had the three elements made? Could he dare to hope it was the Soul of All Things? He felt its power through the glass, and its warmth.

I should lie here and wait, his mind offered. *The tide will rise, all you have to do is wait. Think of how it will lift you, tumble you, back into watery arms.*

Something tugged at his wrist. He looked down to see his bracelet pulling at his skin, vibrating like a tuning fork.

He left the cold water behind, not looking back at the thundering waves. There were new things to see.

He'd reached the purple haze, that mystery on the horizon that Vorax had pointed to for all this time. He could see the wonder that it was made of now. The light came from the thousands of Shadows, constructing forms like bees making honeycomb, but on such a grand scale that the mind boggled. Their work finished, they flew away, wrapping themselves in clouds as they disappeared.

The Pale World *was* a laboratory. It had made all the wonders that he'd seen, and now it had made his city.

London.

With its spires and towers, clocks and rooftops, alleyways and wharfs. The Shadows had captured every detail with devotion. They'd made bricks of every kind and color, paver stones, rippled window glass, wooden beams, and roof shingles.

It was a place for Vorax to feel human, a place of mimicry, and it was a lie. It was Pale London.

Kip walked past the docks and the deserted taverns that lined the edge of the wharf. All with darkened windows. No beer would flow there tonight. No stories and lies would be shared around a fire. No fights would break out in a flash of drunken passion.

Grief had held him in isolation for so long that it took the absence of life for him to remember it. He missed his home with such an aching that he marveled he could stand it. He thought he could see the people on the streets; only ghosts now, only memory.

The fishmonger, the curio shop manager, the tobacconist, Ragman...

The smiling faces, the angry, the apathetic. The man who helped a woman after she tripped on the curb. The haggling that turned to a profanity-laden argument. The girl crying after dropping her penny lick.

All gone.

A ghost world in this underworld.

The echo of his shoes on the cobblestones were muted,

further draining the world of life. Not even sound wanted to penetrate this place.

His bracelet knew where it wanted to go even if Kip didn't. It pulled this way and tugged that way. Muscle memory spurred him on, bringing him to the one place he didn't want to go.

21

The square opened up before him.

The market was abandoned, its sellers gone for the day. They'd packed up their curios and wonders, things that had sailed across seas to get there. Goods from the Orient and the Middle East, spices from India. All the foreign tongues that spoke here had been silenced, leaving only their memory and the longing to hear them again.

It was Potter's Market.

The Three Nymphs fountain was there, a dead landmark in a pale world. No water flowed from its stone spout. Kip remembered throwing a coin in that fountain, making a wish. He wondered now what he had wished for so long ago.

There were empty barrels and crates, usually brimming with mulled ciders or packed with strange root vegetables. There was an empty spot under a stone arch where the Bird Lady took up residence, the silent woman with her collection of cages and the chatter of voices inside, all wanting a taste of freedom.

But it wasn't a vision. It was real.

Kip saw the bulk of a cart being pulled out of the square. It had a canvas tarp over it, hiding its contents. He approached it with caution.

It was the Bird Lady. She was no memory or vision, she was real, as tangible as he was.

"Ma'am, where are you going?" he said. "Do you remember me?"

"Must go," she grunted, straining under her load.

"But...but you're here. You shouldn't be here."

The woman had been alive when he'd left London, and should be there still for all he knew. How did she come to be here? There was no sign of the young girl that played at the folds of her dress while she worked.

Kip reached out his hand, rested it on her arm. He needed to make contact, to know if she was real. He felt the rough fabric of her sleeve and the thin bones of her arm beneath. She looked down at his hand and then up at his face.

"Something coming." There was a sadness in her eyes. She pulled away, turning her back, and left the square. The caged birds beneath the canvas were silent, knowing better than to sing.

Something's coming.

Kip turned back to the abandoned square.

Then he saw.

Enos walked down the steps, into the abandoned marketplace. He was laughing, his head thrown back. His teeth shown like pearls. This was no shade of Enos. It was a window through time, showing the real thing. He moved in a bubble that captured a thriving London, a barrier between this pale version and the real one.

There was another figure in the widening sphere. Kip saw himself, a few steps behind.

It was his turn to be pale, to be nothing.

This other Kip was happy, careless, ignorant. He thought life was a laugh, and that happiness was a guarantee. The boy before him thought life was inevitable.

"God, no," Kip whispered, not wanting to see this vision, wanting to turn away but knowing he couldn't. Here he was, even now, chasing a memory.

It had been a year ago on a crisp autumn night. The stars had burst through the smog of London, demanding to be seen. They were diamonds cut from light. The two had always taken this route back to Alchemy House, passing through the market that they loved.

It was Bonfire Night and they'd gone out to see the burning effigies of Guy Fawkes, and the fireworks that followed. They'd stayed out too late, and drank too heartily. Kip remembered they'd stopped to hear a quartet play for their supper in Finsbury Square. Scarves wrapped tightly around their faces as they played their instruments with fingerless gloves, digits dancing over strings.

Mozart, Offenbach, and Boccherini.

Enos's Boccherini.

With the crescendo of the music, someone ignited an effigy down the street. The gun-powder plot foiled for the two-hundred and seventy-sixth time, England's most famous rebel consumed in flame. The light from the straw scarecrow poured down the street and wrapped the musicians in its glow. It was the synchronicity of vision and sound the Kip remembered. Timing so perfect that it had to be divine.

He'd turned to watch Enos, stealing a glance at his love. His clear eyes caught the firelight as the music flowed over them. That moment should have stayed. It was a perfect sum. There was no need for anything to follow.

Cheers and applause filled the street and the musicians bowed. Kip and Enos put more than their share in a tattered top hat and were happy to see it quickly filling. They turned and left, filled with the magic of that brief moment. All of creation had bent to bring it about and now it had passed.

Alone, they walked down Crown Street then Bishopsgate, then turned down the stairs into the empty marketplace.

Laughing, back in their perfect bubble of light.

Enos walked to the fountain and Kip followed. They watched the gurgling water and pretended they heard voices in its bubbles.

Enos said it was a wishing well.

"I wish," Kip whispered.

He slipped his fingers between Enos's. Their hands intertwined and, leaning forward, Kip kissed him on the cheek. It was the smallest movement, imperceptible compared to all other movements. In a world with ships battered at sea, and trains thundering across continents, with horses marching in processions, and people screaming in parliament, it should have been nearly invisible.

"Oi, look here!"

It was a gruff voice, slurred by too much alcohol, and was soon joined by another.

"Two benders out for a bending stroll."

Four roughs came out of the shadows. Two drank from flasks and one pulled from a cigarette, a tiny pinpoint of red embers in the darkness.

The leader of the group had a green bowler on and

looked the part of whatever role he was playing. Kip wondered how he could take himself so seriously; fit a part that was such a stereotype: the street rough, the brutish masculine bully.

"I'm Kip of Alchemy House," he said, as if titles would matter to the ignorant.

"I heard of you, least ways I've heard of Alchemy House. You're one of them, eh?"

"What are you? A wizard?" another one said.

"No, mate, he's a witch."

"You know what we do to witches?"

The smoking one answered by igniting a match between his fingers, sulfur and flame sparking to life.

"Why don't you two faggots kiss again. Let's see it," the man with the green bowler said.

"You want 'em to kiss, Charlie?"

"Yeah, let's see what all the fuss is about."

Kip looked to Enos. He'd always been defiant in the face of hate, even when it was reckless. Enos refused to shrink from the world and his place in it. He did the one thing that Kip would never have done, he smiled.

"Something funny, poof?" Charlie with the green bowler asked.

The four men had fanned out in a semi-circle around the fountain, spoiling for some action, something to cap the excitement of Bonfire Night.

As if offering them an alternative, a thundering noise split the sky. Shards of colored light filled the air, blotting out the stars with fireworks.

Stabbing embers of red, purple, and blue igniting into flowers.

As they looked up, Kip slipped a hand into his pocket. He'd brought Filament powder to make his own fireworks display. He'd thought he could entrance merry-makers with a light show; flames that danced around rooftops, or spun around lampposts. He'd planned to watch the faces of people in the crowd, to see wonder in their eyes. The magic of alchemy filtering through their minds and inspiring visions.

Now that same alchemy could be a weapon. His fingers found the leather pouch in his pocket and slipped inside, powder coating each digit.

The fireworks exploded above, the punch of each explosion bringing fear instead of excitement. Charlie and his ruffians looked up, their faces masks of color. Kip saw Charlie's hand move to his belt and slowly pull a knife from a thin leather sheath. It looked like a gutting knife for deboning fish, a precise instrument.

There was a break in the light show and the group looked back to their two captives.

"Now kiss, faggots."

Kip brought his hand forward and blew on his palm. Blue flames ignited and flowed from his hand. They shot out in a straight line, stabbing towards one of the men with a flask. The man tried to duck out of the way, but the fire caught the left lapel of his jacket and ignited.

Kip made a long arc with his hand, the flames moving like a whip. The four men jumped back.

I'd only meant to frighten them, he thought. It was a display of power, of dominance; the only thing men like this would understand.

The blade of the knife glinted with the rainbow colors of the fireworks as Charlie moved towards Enos.

At the same moment, the man with the blazing lapel charged forward and caught Kip in the stomach. He pushed him back with his violent embrace until the back of Kip's knees hit the lip of the fountain. They both tumbled into the water, liquid dowsing Kip's flaming hand, and filling his eyes and ears. He heard the muffled *pop* of a firework and then felt strong hands holding him down in the water. Ice cold, it rushed into his mouth as he gasped for air and tried to claw away from his attacker.

Every few seconds there was a reprieve as he was able to get his head above water, just enough time to see Charlie wrestling with Enos and the other men laughing. Enos struggled to get to Kip, even now trying to save him first.

Kip viewed the action like a stuttering film strip, the movements skipping frames with each dunk in the fountain.

Enos grabbing the back of Kip's attacker.

Turning to face Charlie with his sharp knife.

Thrown punches in a flurry of watery motion.

Kip brought his knee up and caught his attacker in the groin, then pushed him to the side. He stood up, water running off him in a torrent.

"STOP!" he screamed.

Charlie had Enos by the head, his giant palm cupping his black hair, thick white fingers running through black.

Kip jumped forward as Charlie forced Enos's head down, cracking it against the side of the fountain. It was like a gunshot that brought people to their senses. The sound made his men stop laughing. It froze Kip in his tracks.

Enos crumbled and fell into the fountain. Kip jumped forward and caught his body, pulling his head above water and cradling it in his arms. Blood pumped from his skull and spilled into the fountain. It ran between Kip's fingers as he tried to find the wound and stop the bleeding. Tears stung his eyes and blurred his vision as he began to mumble.

"You're all right. You're all right."

He said it like a mantra as he rocked back and forth.

Charlie's men ran, disappearing into the night. Charlie looked on for a moment, standing like a lost child in a crowd. He opened his mouth to say something, then turned and ran.

"You're okay, my love," Kip whispered.

A second wave of fireworks lit the sky, throwing color onto Enos's face; turning the fountain water blue, then red, then purple.

How could there be so much blood? How could life be contained in this unremarkable liquid, the fuel that powered a human being?

If I hadn't held his hand, Kip thought, his eyes blurred with tears. *If I hadn't been so stupid, so careless. If I'd only been content with a secret.*

If only I hadn't kissed him on the cheek. One small gesture that had brought down the avalanche and changed the course of two lives.

If I hadn't used alchemy to defend us. If only I'd been content to take a beating, satisfied by each blow.

Enos opened his eyes. They looked past Kip, reflecting the colors in the sky.

"Kip," he whispered.

It was his last word.

There was nothing grand that took Enos from him. There was no epic meaning, no import. It was a pedestrian death, if a death could be called that. It was as common as any other violence, and just as final.

Kip watched all this again with horror. It was so familiar now that it felt like a part of him. It might have been tattooed on his flesh for all to see.

He watched himself cradle Enos's dead body. His lifeblood spilled into the fountain and swirled with the water creating small whirlpools of red.

Then something else came forward.

A thin stream of watery light flowed from Enos's cracked skull, like a piece of liquid silver. It shimmered in the water, changing from blue to white, its refractions like small spider webs knitting together below the surface. The fountain was illuminated as the light filled it.

Kip stepped forward. They were the most difficult steps he'd ever taken, returning to the scene that had torn down all the structures of his life; having to be a witness to violence once again, and his part in it. He'd returned to the looping horror that had cycled in his memory for every second of every day.

Kip's shade looked up, still cradling Enos's head. His love's eyes were still open, two glassy orbs looking up to the sky.

Kip and his shade perceived one another. Kip felt like he was seeing himself in a dream. He knew it wasn't real even though it felt so vital, so tangible. And, just like a dream, it broke the order of reality.

"You're all right," Kip said. "Somehow you're going to be all right."

He looked down at the silver strands stirring in the water, and then stepped into the fountain. Kip knelt beside his own shade, helping to hold Enos's body. They remained there in silence for a moment, as if saying a prayer.

Is this the moment of significance? Kip found it impossible to think clearly, his mind as muddled as the fountain water; his thoughts swirling in disparate patterns, disturbed like still water being broken by a stone.

Kip reached into his jacket and pulled out the vial. The small orbs of light still danced behind the glass, their constant movement sometimes joining them together and then pulling them apart again. He shook the vial and watched the elements combine once again. They flashed and sparkled, happy to be mixed.

He brought the vial to Enos's lips, marveling how quickly flesh could be deadened, how it could change to a lifeless thing. Tilting the vial, he watched the liquid slide into his mouth, illuminating it from the inside like a fire in a cave.

Surely this was the moment. He'd mined this dark world for its materials and brought something forth. He'd suffered for this. If there was meaning to anything he would find it here.

He waited for the light to flow back into Enos's skull, for the ragged bones of the fracture to heal, and for his eyes to fill with life again. A gasp of breath and then a joyful reunion. Flowing tears, and declarations and apologies made. Then the work of building a new life could begin, together.

Nothing.

The liquid disappeared from Enos's lips and slipped down his throat. It was inert, just another useless parlor trick with no magic behind it.

Kip thought of Blackmoor. Never had he wished so intensely to have his powers. Magic instead of reason.

I've failed completely then, Kip thought. Mercury, salt, and sulfur; he'd collected the three essences and it had made nothing.

The Kip shade had backed away, moving to the ledge of the fountain where he sat with his head in his hands. His form flickered as if his body couldn't contain his sorrow and it threatened to snuff him out.

Kip lowered Enos's body into the water gently and let him float there. He too, had started to fade. Pale London couldn't sustain the memory. It needed to purge all reality.

Kip eyed the silver streaks in the water. It was the last bit of Enos he might ever see. A sudden greed for the silver overcame him, a need to have it as keepsake, safe behind glass.

He dipped the vial into the water, careful not to spill out any more of the contents. The strands of light were drawn to it immediately. They spiraled towards the glass and mingled with the glowing liquid that remained. What this new element added to the mix, Kip couldn't be sure, but it had excited the other materials. The glass vibrated faintly as he quickly corked it.

Was it the life-entire of his beloved? What stories were imprinted in this substance?

Enos's body was transparent now. It merged with the water and then vanished completely, taking the light from the fountain with it.

Goodbye again, Kip thought.

He stood up and filled his lungs with the chilly air. The fireworks were silenced, the vision had ended.

He turned to face his shade. The poor weeping thing was nearly bent in half, as if he were trying to hide himself from himself. His body flickered and prepared to vanish.

"Wait!" Kip commanded. "I'm not done with you yet."

He looked at his weeping shade and remembered all his nights bent over in sorrow, unable to move or to think. He looked at the fountain, *the well*; the wide circle of its mouth so familiar. He thought of the one place that had given him solace, wrapped in stone and timber. The place where it had all begun.

22

The door swung open, spilling dull light into darkness.

The Shadows had done their work, making the Alchemy House of Pale London identical to the real thing. It was just as dead as the rest of the city, but not for lack of details.

Kip climbed the two steps to the foyer and looked through the forest of branches that created a tunnel to the living room. He'd almost missed seeing them, even after all that had happened. The bizarre seed that he'd planted that had grown into a monster.

I cracked the edges of the world somehow.

The Kip shade followed as he walked through his home, now silent as a mausoleum. His books were all there, no doubt filled with empty pages. The baubles and trinkets that one collected during a lifetime were sat on their shelves, peering out from the nooks and corners they'd been placed in. A thin layer of dust covered them like settled ash after a fire.

His eyes moved over all the objects that made a home; the things that planted him to one spot in the world, saying, *this is my place. Whatever comes, I will face it here.*

The hearth was a dark hole. Kip went to it hoping to feel some invisible warmth and the memories that came with it; nights spent peering into flames and trying to read their messages.

He crawled forward, towards the one place that called to him like a beacon. The stone back of the hearth pushed aside with a heavy scrapping sound, and he continued to crawl, inching his way through the darkness. His shade followed, the scuffling sounds of his movements muted and distant.

Stand up, his mind barked, and he obeyed. He got to his feet and walked without needing a prop. What room did he know better in the entire world than this basement and the things in it?

A glowing light appeared. Rippling patterns flooded the wall as he moved forward. He came to the wooden staircase. It had been restored by the Shadows, a balcony to peer down into his laboratory and its secrets.

His heart raced when he saw the well. It was still there waiting for him with all its whispered secrets hidden in its dark center. But it too had changed.

A golden light filled the room, its soft glow illuminating the bedrock of the walls and ceiling and the dirt of the floor. Its light tangled in the branches, casting shadows that looked like dark veins.

I wished for this well back in London, I willed it to be. And now I've wished again and I've got an answer. But what had he wished for?

Kip descended the steps, their wood creaking under his

weight. His feet hit the dirt floor and again he wanted to feel the earth between his toes, to be anchored to this place, to plant himself here like one of the branches.

His shade stayed behind, watching cautiously from the steps as Kip approached the well. His hand touched the stone. Instead of the dull coldness he'd expected, he was met with warmth.

I poured my soul into this well, bit by bit. I drained my lifeblood, spilled it into this memory hole, and here it is, preserved in amber. Look how it glows and moves. It was here all along, wrapped in memory, and almost forgotten.

How greedy to want anything else, how vain; given the greatest gift of creation and shunning it because it doesn't last forever.

Kip felt a force move in him with something close to euphoria. A golden hue tinted his sight, like looking at a sunrise. Beams of yellow light rippled across a landscape he didn't recognize.

The landscape faded and new visions appeared. They moved in a flurry, streaming by like water beneath a bridge. There were moments of intense joy and sorrow and every gradation in-between.

The visions triggered emotions in Kip that he thought had been deadened or had never existed. They moved so quickly that he couldn't identify them. Perhaps to name them would only diminish them. Names were static things. They didn't account for change, for evolution. Simply calling the substance in the well "light," was an insult to something so moving.

So moving it was perilous.

Was it the past, present, or future? He didn't know.

Perhaps it was this moment, begging to be appreciated, begging for him to open his eyes once and for all.

The light grew as if in response. It spilled over the lip of the well, dancing over his hands and down to the floor. He thought he could see through the bedrock, to some infinite depth below.

In his London, the well had been a passageway to death; here it was the opposite. Here it wanted to sing, and celebrate, and heal, and recover lost things.

Kip had the one ingredient that would let it do that.

He held the vial in his hand and watched it catch the light. Mercury, salt, and sulfur mixed with the soul of Enos.

He held the glass tube up and then tipped it over the well. The thin spindles of light moved down, half-falling, half-floating.

The well took it. Not with greed or hunger.

The light rallied, like a choir of voices. The gold wove together and punched upwards. It pierced the bones of the house, a spotlight that carved through matter. It shed the dead skin of Alchemy House, boring a hole through its center.

Kip saw the outline of floorboards, branches, and timbers, and then straight to a sky above. The light moved up through the tower of Alchemy House, shattering each of its four windows. He heard the crispness of the breaking glass, tiny bells on the wind.

"The Soul of all Things," he said.

His shade watched from the stairs, clutching the wooden bannister. He looked horrified.

But Kip wasn't afraid. The broken frame of the house let the air in. It was the crisp smell of autumn that brought hope and nostalgia, tangled together. He looked down into the well again and saw things that the mind couldn't articulate or comprehend.

He thought, *all beauty is melancholy. All of life is autumn.*

And he saw a deeper truth. Beneath all the wonderment, beneath the glowing light and visions, at a depth greater than the spectacle of this world, there was a truth. It was uncompromising but not stern, just a simple fact that he had chosen to ignore again and again.

The dead stayed dead.

The universe had its alchemy, too. It was the alchemy of all creation and, just like a matchstick, it could flare to life, burning brightly before burning out. Did that lessen its warmth? Did that diminish its power?

Kip looked up at his shade, still crouched on the stairs.

"It's what I suspected all along," he said. "It's what I knew in my heart."

His shade nodded, almost imperceptibly.

Kip held the now empty vial in his hand and looked back to the golden light in the well. He dipped the glass tube into the gold, its viscous liquid filled the vial. A small universe hung suspended in the light. It shown through his hand. He saw the network of veins there, the blood pumping, the bones moving. He saw the elongated cells that made his muscles and the delicate folds of skin that made his fingerprints.

He corked the vial and slipped it into his breast pocket.

It was nearly impossible to turn away from the well, but Kip did. He felt its warmth on his back as he walked to the stairs. His shade stood to follow him. Together they left the basement.

The hearth seemed colder than before and the room less real. Whatever magic sold the illusion of this world had faded. There was a snaking crack in the wall from the explosion of light. Pieces of sky were visible between the broken chunks of plaster and wood.

The two Kips stood silently, both in thought.

Kip faced his shade.

"It's time to end this, time to go home."

He turned to the front door.

An envelope sat on the doorstep, the wind through the open door tugging at its edges. Kip walked over and picked it up, turned it in his hands, felt the echo of the past. He had done this before in another lifetime.

A thick black seal of messy wax sealed the envelope. He broke it with his thumb and pulled out a piece of crisp parchment. Scanning the words, he wanted to laugh over the mock politeness. Vorax believed in decorum, if nothing else; even if it was playacting, even if he was an ape that had learned to talk.

"It's an invitation," Kip said, "from Dark House."

23

Kip and his shade stepped outside into a world that seemed brighter than before. He looked up, squinting at the ruined tower of Alchemy House with its shattered roof and walls and the fading glow of the light that had gutted the structure.

The tower lingered in the atmosphere above, slowly absorbed by the gray that covered Pale London.

A tapping sound on the cobblestones made Kip look down. There was an old man hunched against the outside wall of Alchemy House. He drew the darkness around him, calling it from every angle until it pooled at his feet.

The tapping came from a smooth piece of driftwood that he used as a prop. He clutched it in a white hand, more bone than flesh. Arthritic knuckles held it awkwardly. The darkness fled as the old man stood up, his back hunched as he rose to unsteady feet.

"I thought I'd find you here, boy," Lord Blackmoor said in a rasping whisper. "I knew you'd come eventually, back to your cave. I searched this entire city for answers. It's a hollow replica with no meaning, nothing but mockery, and no sign of the only place I want to get to."

Dark House.

The old man was ruined. In the short time since they'd been on the ship, he'd been stripped of whatever life he'd had left. His body looked like it was pulling into itself, taking away every bit of vitality.

Still, Kip could see the fury behind his eyes.

"You brought it to life, boy. I saw it in your eyes. You went blind staring at Dark House. It's the hub of the world, don't you see? Find it and we could kill Vorax. We could control everything."

"That's your dream, not mine."

"Why does this world not affect you?" Blackmoor asked, half-sneering, half in desperation. "What wretched alchemy did you use?"

He saw the shade at his side, Kip's twin, taking in this new oddity without comment.

"You said it yourself, Blackmoor. I made this place. I willed this dead world to life."

Lord Blackmoor's fury consumed him, rippling over his face in waves. He no longer looked like a lord, but a beggar.

Voices echoed down the street. Kip turned to see Britten and Fairfield coming towards them. They chattered nervously as they came, lost in some argument.

They stopped short as they saw the gathering outside of Alchemy House: Kip, his shade, and an old man.

"We...we need to get to Surrey," Fairfield said.

"A ship is waiting for us there," Britten added. "I don't know where it's going, but it calls to us."

The Pale World was a loop. Kip wanted to stop them, feeling a sudden swell of pity.

"You don't have to go," he said. "Lord Blackmoor set this in motion. He sent your shades to die on the bottom of the ocean."

"Did he?" Fairfield asked. "I don't remember."

Then he turned to the old man. At first he took him in without recognition, his face neutral as he greeted a stranger, then his eyes widened. Amelia Britten let out a pained gasp.

"You," she muttered. "You did this to us."

Words spilled from her like water coming from a drain spout.

"I had a life; passions, loves, hatreds. I had a child waiting for me in Somerset, waiting for her grandmother to return. You had no right!"

The spiritualist raged and her body flickered like a candle. The threads that tied the Pale World together were coming undone.

Fairfield joined in, adding to her diatribe.

"Arrogant old man. You sit at the head of a house and think it means you run the world. I had a life I don't even remember, except in shades. It's madness to feel only loss and not know why."

Lord Blackmoor just smiled. His mouth split to show missing and dead teeth.

"Small people with small ideas. I told you this at our last meeting. I told you the arc of the world and the direction it would bend. I told you I could tame the stars themselves; call them down to consume you. And I will do it again."

Blackmoor's eyes turned to red ember as Britten and Fairfield lunged forward. They grabbed the old man, pushing him backwards. His driftwood cane clattered to the ground and skidded across cobblestones. They tore at his body, rending clothes and scratching flesh. The old man didn't seem to notice as he spoke.

"*Primum Dominum!*"

A cracking sound filled the sky above, the air breaking like glass. He was using the last bit of his power, the power he didn't dare use on the ship. Shards of stars descended. They struck what remained of the Alchemy House tower, cutting through it like paper. The structure moaned and then rolled to one side before falling.

The tower fell on Blackmoor, Britten and Fairfield like a hammer striking. The ground shook, sending out waves of energy as a ruin of wood and stone entombed them.

The force threw Kip backwards. On his back, he looked up at the gray sky and the smoke streaming overhead.

A splinter of wood stuck out of his arm. He gently pulled it out and felt the blood flow from the hole it had made. The vial in his pocket vibrated.

He looked at the wreckage of his home; his memories, his entire life shattered in a heap.

As he got up, he saw his shade running away.

"Our work's not done!" he yelled.

They had to finish this together, he knew that now. This scared, delicate part of him had to share the ending.

Kip ran after him.

The shade phased in and out as it ran, stumbling over cobblestones. It darted ahead, teleporting a few feet at a time as it decided if it should stay or go.

He wants to go back to the Three Nymphs Fountain, he thought. *To die in the shallow water or to stare into it for all eternity.*

A lighting strike cut the air behind them. It rippled over Pale London, moving down the streets and through buildings. Laughter mingled with the light, an old man's cackle.

As the thunderclap rolled away, a grinding sound replaced it.

Kip looked back. His shade, too, was transfixed.

The rubble of Alchemy House shifted. It groaned like a beast, then began to move.

Wooden beams shuddered from the wreckage, their ends joining together forming an armature. A red light wove in and out of every space like a mouse darting from hole to hole. It was a demolition moving in reverse.

Ceiling beams bent to make a ribcage, an empty void where the heart should have been.

Black shingles flew over the skeleton like bats, covering it in scales.

Large stones rolled up wooden arms until they settled into a head-shape. Two black pits for eyes.

My hearth.

Kip was transfixed by it. He knew he should run or scream but he was frozen.

Then a voice boomed.

"Kip of Alchemy House!" it said as the head ignited. Flames leapt into the eyes and bled through the mouth. It opened its jaw, showing broken glass teeth, each one catching the light.

The giant shook off the rubble and got to its feet, the last bits of it all flying into place.

And it laughed, a broken glass laugh.

Dust fell from its body as it looked around, taking in Pale London with two stone eyes.

Standing beneath it was Lord Blackmoor. He was the engine driving it.

Kip's shade turned and ran again.

"I'm not done with you yet!" he yelled after it.

The monster roared and another shockwave moved over the city. As it rolled away, it was answered with a tinkling sound like a thousand tiny bells.

Glass stripped away from every window frame, pulled out like extracted teeth. The shards met in the air and danced in circles before focusing on their target. They followed Kip with a terrifying precision.

The magician was coming, wrapped in a lurching giant. The glass buzzed overhead, an army moving ahead of its commander.

The first wave of glass raced forward, whistling through the air. Kip caught up to his shade and pushed him forward, gripping him tightly by the arm.

"Don't look back!" he yelled over the deafening buzz.

They ran down the street, a boy and his double, looking for some way to escape. Kip forced his shade down an alley-way, just as a thousand glass teeth caught up with them. The splinters hammered the timbered side of a building where Kip had just been a moment before, shredding wood and impaling stone.

The alley was no more than three feet wide, forcing them to run in single file. Glass broke above them and rained down with a musical timbre that was almost pleasant. Kip put his hands up to protect himself.

They ran on and on, just escaping each wave of attack. The glass moved like a patrolling army, some following from behind while others snaked down adjacent streets, trying to cut them off. The hollow windows of Pale London looked on, gaping eye sockets watching a fox hunt.

Kip didn't know how long they'd run but the streets were

suddenly familiar again. Chiswell Street, Royal Street, and straight on to Magic House.

The alleyway widened like a river meeting the sea; the vast courtyard that preceded the magician's house leaving them exposed. A wave of glass swept over the tops of buildings and froze in the air, each point trained on Kip and his shade.

The giant's booming footsteps echoed across the square.

Its head came into view, peaking over the rooftops. It spotted Kip and its eyes flared. Rushing ahead, it crashed through a row of buildings, turning them to pulp. The wreckage spilled into the square. The creature stepped over it and stretched to its full height. Its fire eyes exploded, cutting sharp shadows and dimming the rest of the world.

Kip turned to his shade. "No more running. Never again."

The vial in his pocket was a heartbeat now. It pumped with a steady rhythm.

A figure approached through the wreckage.

Lord Francis Blackmoor emerged from the shadows. His chest heaved as he tried to catch his breath. A thin track of blood ran from his mouth and he dabbed at it with the back of his hand. He came like a bag of bones, clattering over every cobblestone.

"Strange that fate would bring us back here, no?"

He looked over Kip's shoulder at his darkened home, its light extinguished as it faded into the gray sky. The giant followed his gaze, Alchemy House looking at Magic House.

Another wave of glass came up from behind Kip, until they was completely surrounded. The shards moved slowly as if they were breathing, gently rising and falling, and waiting for their master's command.

Blackmoor smiled his sick toothless smile.

"What is an alchemist without his tools? No potions and tinctures to save you now, boy. How impotent you are."

He extended a withered hand.

"Give me that invitation to Dark House."

Kip shook his head.

"You weren't invited."

Blackmoor's smile widened and for a moment, Kip saw him as he had been in the world. The man who had entertained royalty and dazzled London with his abilities. It was the last time anyone would see him like that, the last time any good memory would outweigh the bad. Somewhere his heart had turned black.

"Then die, Alchemist, as you should have long ago. Die as all broken things should. Join your perverted friend. You built this place for him, after all."

Blackmoor closed his eyes. The ember fire burned beneath his eyelids, casting its terrible light. The giant's eyes burned too, turning its stone head to molten rock. It dripped in waves from the eye sockets, two long red tears.

Kip felt a heartbeat.

The creature screamed. Glass razors shot from its mouth. It lunged forward. Arms outstretched, fingers clawed. It looked like it was going to embrace him. The army of glass shards followed, closing in a tight circle.

Kip imagined the glass shredding his body, ripping through clothes, then flesh, then bone. The blades would denude him down to nothing. There would be an ending, a final ending. Blackmoor would dig through the scraps to find the invitation he so desperately wanted.

Kip stood his ground. He reached out a hand and

grabbed his shade's arm. It was like grabbing a shadow, but he held on.

Something moved in his chest. It was a single thumping beat that brought a spasm of pain. His hand went to his vest pocket and found the vial there. A golden light pulsed from it, moving through his hand and racing outward in a perfect sphere.

Screaming, the giant closed the distance, its body slamming into the circle of light. Its scream of rage turned to one of pain.

Blackmoor fell to one knee with a gasp.

The light carved into the giant. Its arms tried to grab it, desperate to find Kip and crush him. The glass blades met the light in a furious collision. They sparked like small fireworks. The air filled with a thousand sharp popping sounds as Blackmoor's weapons were destroyed one by one.

The old man watched as his work was rendered useless. All the glass in Pale London flowed into the sphere and was obliterated.

Kip turned to his shade to see the look of horror on his face.

"Don't be afraid anymore," he said.

The giant howled as it tried to reach him. Alchemy House disintegrated around him. He saw flashes of his old life go by, pieces of his home that were now part of this monster. A grasping hand reached towards him as its fingers burned away to nothing.

And then it was over.

The final spark of evaporating glass gave way to a cloud of dust. It swirled around them, filling the square before drifting over rooftops and out of sight.

The golden light contracted back into Kip's pocket, leaving only a slight vibration.

Lord Blackmoor let his driftwood cane drop to the ground. It bounced over cobblestones before coming to rest. Whatever life had fueled him for this last lap had left him. Age had caught up with him.

He fell to his knees, a look of sorrow on his face.

"I just wanted..."

His voice trailed into silence as his body swayed, pushed by some invisible force. He looked up at Kip.

"Help me get to Dark House, boy. It's the only thing that can save me. It's the end point on the map. Help me get there."

His breath labored as if it were being pulled through a cloth. It came in waves, each one farther apart than the next.

He was looking at the middle space between Magic House and the sky above. His eyes widened. Kip turned and saw nothing but the gray roof of Magic House and the stars peeking through a pale sky. But the magician was transfixed by some private sight.

"Oh, God. It's beautiful," he said, with more horror than wonder.

Lord Francis Blackmoor fell forward, his head hitting the ground with a soft thud, and died.

24

Kip looked at Blackmoor's body. He took in the stillness of it. He felt a hint of pity, even now. The driftwood cane had rolled a few feet away and still wobbled back and forth on the uneven ground. Then, it too, stopped.

His shade was transfixed by the dead magician, his watery eyes taking in the sight.

"Come," Kip said, as he turned and faced the wide square; Magic House waited at the other side, and something else. The air had turned electric.

His heels clicked on cobblestones; cobblestones that had paved the way for beggars and kings, whores and maidens, and all the residents of London in the long arc of history. Here in Pale London, who knew what else had walked these streets?

He turned his head to see the door to Magic House open. Britten and Fairfield walked down the stairs. They didn't see him, maybe they couldn't. They were paler than ever, merely a hint of two people. They had their loop to run, their boat waiting for them in Surrey. Kip was going to end all loops.

Goodbye, Britten. Goodbye, Fairfield. Lost souls like me, he thought.

But something in him resisted self-pity. There was a whisper inside that began to speak, to raise its voice until it was an exclamation.

Kip pulled the vial from his pocket and held it up, the light of it bleeding through his fingers. It refracted off of every surface, dazzling the stones at his feet. The world was transformed by its light. Its warmth bled into his hand and moved up his arm until it settled in his chest, where he hoped it would stay.

The structure of Magic House loomed in the mist ahead, looking less fearsome now. It was dead just like its master. Kip could see the stained-glass dome of the dining room ceiling, its glass darkened. The flood of memory came, bringing with it images that now seemed so distant.

The half-remembered life he had once had. He felt the arc lights of Blackmoor's imprisonment and the endless stars above. Shadow was curled at his feet, happy to sit near a fire, happy to listen and learn. Drinks imbibed, food eaten, knowledge shared.

But Kip wasn't here for Magic House or its memory. He looked up as a bell sounded, *the* bell. He was so close to it now he thought it would deafen him. It was a sound that could crack stone. The ripple of its noise was visible in the night sky, blurring the stars as a wave moved out in all directions.

The sound was above Magic House, but it was anchored to something, something that had remained just out of sight in the real London, hidden from all the gawking stares and questioning minds.

It was Dark House.

As the bell faded, its structure became visible; built on the back of Magic House but made to eclipse it. It was a monstrous thing, beautiful but unknowable. Walls and rooflines appeared as they traced an outline in the sky, like a blueprint pulled from a drafting table.

Kip saw now what it was, every angle, every vertex and line, was mapped to a constellation. It could only be seen from one vantage point, presumably at one time, under one night sky. He looked up at the stars, lost in their patterns. This was no night sky that London had ever seen.

The patterns wove together and brought Dark House to life. It had many steep gables poking from the rooftop like a bottom row of teeth, each one with a sunken window in it. Something moved behind each pane of glass, or many restless things that had waited for this moment to be seen. There were towers on each end of the house and one in the center that rose above the rest.

The main tower climbed into the sky, its flat black walls made of a deeper part of night. The tower abandoned the map of constellations and found its own shape; maybe something far from earth, far from their solar system. It wanted to be looked at, after all this time, it wanted to be perceived.

At the pinnacle of the tower was a clock, if something so abstract could be called a clock. It had a circular face that shimmered between two and three dimensions, first a flat circle then a globe of light. There were no hands but a series of moving arcs of light that wove themselves into different patterns.

It's not measuring time, Kip thought. *Or, at least, not a time measured in minutes and hours. Nothing so mundane as linear time with its one marching direction.*

Kip held the vial up, letting its light shine out. It spilled onto the faint outline of a giant double-door, the light giving it shape. Dark House accepted the gift with a low rumble and the doors began to grind open, moving outward.

They opened wide, a darker spot in a wall of constellations.

Kip took a deep breath and entered.

25

Blackness surrounded him. It felt organic, a thin membrane he could almost touch, but if he tried, it slinked away, leading him farther on.

It led him through a maze, now turning right, now pushing straight ahead, each choice pre-ordained. Each turn brought an emotion, until Kip felt as if he'd left his body and was free to wander, free to re-live forgotten memories and fantasies. They mixed together in a sweet but painful concoction.

There was his first sight, far too bright and tinged with red.

With blood.

Muscles stretched, lungs inhaled. Every fiber was tested for strength. How far could this form be pushed? What great things could it do? What hurts could it sustain?

Now there was emotion and it swelled and rallied with double the fierceness, bringing things wanted and unwanted.

Love begins with Mother and Father, then twists and turns and mutates into something; sometimes beautiful, sometimes not. But it starts there with a single seed and life makes it grow. Every decision adds a branch or a leaf, or sometimes a flower. Those same decisions are shears that can cut away the growth, or a drought that can choke the plant to death.

Maybe it's perennial, Kip thought. *Maybe it can come back even after a fire.*

I left them behind long ago, abandoned and cast out. I found my own way in this world. But what way had he found? A lost love, an obsession, and the mastery of a house he didn't deserve. If all his decisions had brought him to this point, what was their value? If he had gone right each time he should have gone left, what was the purpose?

Kip put his hand out, groping for some support and felt a wall push back against his palm. He steadied himself but immediately pulled his hand away, hating the sensation. It was like a liquid without any wetness, always moving, struggling against some unseen force.

There was a staircase ahead of him and he lurched towards it, trying to move forward no matter what direction. Something moved down the wall and then stopped at the top of the stairs to look back. Two purple eyes trained on him.

He wanted to call out, to see if this was his Shadow, but something stopped him.

Push on, a voice said.

He was at the top of a staircase. It opened up, a wide and grand thing that flared out at the bottom. These were stairs to make an entrance on, but what pomp and circumstance would take place here? It was not a place for celebration.

As he descended the staircase, whatever had fogged his eyes began to clear.

What stood before him boggled the mind. It was the great hall of Dark House.

Huge columns lined the hall. From a distance they looked like stone but the marbled pattern on their surface moved slowly, rising upwards. As Kip stepped closer he saw what looked like the milky pattern of a nebula or star system, always in flux. It spiraled up until it blended with buttresses and beams that were also made of stars, the structures only visible when he walked forward.

The floor of the vast hallway was paved with stones, each one carved with words.

"Tombstones," he whispered.

A nearly endless collection of names and lifespans, all huddled together and worn down by many footfalls. The names and dates jumped out at him, each one telling a story that he'd never hear.

450 B.C.

1066 A.D.

1442 A.D.

1821 A.D.

3044 A.D.

Abantes. Zhao Buwei Fa. Badru Bahati. Sally Archer Callum. Matthew Wright.

Would his name be marked here someday? Would it be written on the stones for others to read?

A light grew at the end of the hall like morning sun through a lifting fog. The expanse of Dark House stretched out before him, too big to take in.

But intimate somehow.

Kip looked up to see the inside of the clock tower. Arcs of light shed from its inner walls, dancing inside it before merging back into place. The underbelly of the massive clock burned like a sun.

A watchful eye keeping time.

26

V orax sat on his throne and watched the boy come.
He looked so frail to him now, a tiny ant
making his way across the landscape. Yet he had
done something wonderful. He had unlocked some secret
that only an alchemist could have. He'd made this inert
world come to life.

The throne was a map of stars. It had just enough form
to support him, phasing in and out as needed, moving with
the shifting of his body. It grew out of a raised dais at the end
of the hall of tombstones.

It was the seat from which Vorax could see the world,
stretching out behind the boy, the spires of Pale London and
the Pale World beyond. Soon it would be his seat to see the
real world, control the greater house of London and reveal
himself to humankind.

The boy's shadow creature sat on the floor next to the
throne, two purple eyes staring out of his cat-like head. The
thing sat stone-still, waiting patiently for his next command.

The boy reached the dais and stood before him.

"You came to me, Master Kip," Vorax said. "You stripped yourself of everything and came to me. Free of your life that came before. Free of everything."

Vorax's eyes flitted to the vial in Kip's hand.

"And you found it. I knew this world could still yield wonders."

He reached down and ran his dark hand over Shadow's back. He could see this rankled the boy and it made him glad.

"You befriended something that wasn't meant for you. One mistake after another brought you here, boy. Meditating on forces greater than your comprehension, you invited death and were then surprised when it accepted."

He snapped his fingers and a shape stirred on the opposite side of the throne.

The shade of Enos stepped forward, as pale and lost as ever.

"What do you think of my new companions?"

Still there was silence from the boy.

"And what do you think of my new house?"

Vorax gestured to the rotating stars behind him as they moved over the spires of Dark House.

"It seemed fitting that we be among the stars. It is, after all, where all mortals are bound. When the sun consumes the earth and pulverizes it into ash and char, the atoms that make your body will rejoin the universe, freed from their cages of flesh. Perhaps you'll be of some use then."

"What is this place?" the boy asked.

The question troubled Vorax. Even now, could the boy not see?

"If Alchemy House is reason and Magic House, mysticism, Dark House is the realm of the unknowable; a place that defies your observing eye. It is the answer to the questions you haven't thought to ask. I am suited to such a place. Imagine this house punching through to your world, a beetle on the back of London, and me at its center.

"Oh, the talk that would inspire, the new ideas that would trigger. Would they come to see the great Vorax, just as you have come? But not to a well in a basement, but to a throne room."

His eyes were drawn to the vial in Kip's hand again and the sweet glow there.

"Come forward."

The alchemist climbed the three steps of the dais and Vorax rose to meet him, the throne pulsing and moving behind him. His two bookends, Shadow and Enos, stayed behind, watching without reaction.

"I can feel the old man is gone. Some vestige of him stirs inside me. The old fool rattled the cage one last time before his end, but only I remain now. He wanted Dark House more than anything. It gives me pleasure to deprive him of that."

Lord Blackmoor was nothing more than a slight vibration now, like a muscle twitching before going still.

"Have you come to deliver the Soul of All Things?"

The boy nodded, and again his calmness niggled Vorax. He wanted this moment to have an intensity, an importance. This was supposed to mean something.

Vorax couldn't take his eyes off the golden liquid. What a sweet wine, how it pulsed and flowed and asked to be consumed.

"Every king has a taste-tester, a servant willing to die for him. You will be mine, Kip. Taste the king's wine for me. Show me your loyalty.

"And if it works for me, we'll resurrect your dear Enos. I

don't want you to think I'm a cruel thing. I keep my promises. You'll see him again; feel his warmth and hear his voice.

"What did you call him when we met? Your raven-haired Boccherini-lover? Your ship-builder and muse and the force that drove you to near-madness. The siren that sang you to this moment, and you can have him back again."

But promise or not, it was a lie. Nothing came back from the dead. That door closed with a finality that couldn't be reversed. The dead tumbled through this place on to their next adventure. And the ones that stayed were nothing but ghosts.

Vorax extended his hand as if he were the one offering the elixir to an eager guest.

"Drink now, Master Kip. Drink and think of your love."

Kip nodded, raised the vial, and then brought it to his lips. The golden liquid slid down his throat, illuminating muscle and bone.

The boy put his head back and closed his eyes. Part of Vorax wondered at his vulnerability, so calmly exposing himself like an animal exposing its belly. Another part of him was entranced by it. He wondered if he'd ever looked so peaceful, if he had known such tranquility. All his existence had been filled with longing and here was a creature that had shed those things.

The glow filled the boy's body now. It came from every pore, breaching his skin as if it were made of wax, a candle burning inside it. Vorax felt himself absorbing whatever power was shed. It came off in waves and just the hint of it nearly drove him mad with longing.

A covetous flame sprang up inside him and he could wait no longer.

Vorax stepped forward and grabbed the vial just as it fell from Kip's open hand. It hit his palm with a delicate *thud* and burned with a sweetness that crept up his arm.

He brought it to his lips as the light filled his mouth, and tipped the liquid back. More of the burning sweetness and then a pause.

First there was nothing. Vorax's mind raced, his eyes darting as he scanned the confines of his body. How long had he waited for this? Even he didn't know. Millennia had crawled by in nothing but darkness with no meter to gauge the time. Silence and waiting was all he had ever known until this, his great experiment.

He'd watched the dead tumble by in an unending line, bound to some new place he couldn't follow. Most came alone, moving to a distant shore, but others came in groups of twos and threes, sometimes dozens. Some held hands, or embraced as they sped by, but most were solitary and lost in some state of puzzlement. They wondered how this had happened to them. Surely they would have been spared the indignity of death. Death was something for others to face, something you could outwit; escape the jaws of the wolf.

And then they were gone, gone to some new place. They faded into a world beyond, that Vorax couldn't follow.

A tickling sensation surged throughout his body. His form, itself so new, was coming to life, soaking up Kip's tonic with greedy slurps. He held up his hands and saw golden light threading itself through his skin. Were there veins forming, the pathways that would deliver life to every molecule? Would he be given a heart, that symbol that had come to mean so much? Life, love, passion, blood.

He looked at Kip, a few steps ahead in the process, his body glowing with more intensity. A sunrise took over his shape, hiding his features in its light. The boy was an engine of life. His light hit the walls of Dark House and brought life even to the dead stone.

It is divine, Vorax thought.

A beat hammered his chest, first a single thump, then followed by another and another; so much like a drum. He brought a hand to his chest and felt the gentle rhythm, nearly gasping with each beat. Light swirled in his breast, a tiny cosmos of gold.

Such wealth these humans carried around with them and they never even realized it, too busy scrapping by for lesser metals, for attention, and all the unrequited things of their world. *Fools, fucking fools.*

Vorax looked at the boy and saw colors he'd never seen before. The gold had swirled into his eyes like ink into water. It brought something new. Had Kip's hair always been so red, his eyes so green? Dark House, too, was a maze of color now. The buttresses and arches of light rose into the night sky and vibrated with life.

"You walk around with this?" He said to Kip, his voice raised as if speaking over music.

The boy nodded.

"And yet you mourn and pout? What a waste, Master Kip. What a waste."

Then something changed.

A shadow crossed the boy's face, or rather, slipped through him, interrupting the golden light. Kip's head snapped to the side, his neck craning in a hideous way. As his head turned, Vorax saw white bone where his head had been split. A sharp geyser of blood issued from the wound, the blood flecked with golden light.

The boy stumbled, then righted himself. His eyes rolled

back in his head as he struggled to stay conscious. He was waiting for something.

There was music. It was both beautiful and malevolent. Kip succumbed to some death, some dark alchemy that Vorax had missed.

He watched in horror and uttered a single word.

"No."

27

Kip descended the steps into the great hall of
Dark House, truly meant for a grand entrance.
He walked slowly down the center, his eyes on
the drama unfolding in front of him.

He saw his shade on the dais, or rather, himself. *It was
always me*, he thought. Just another part of me, one frozen
moment in time that had long since passed. It was a moment
he'd held too tightly and with some sick glee that he didn't
recognize any longer.

Kill that part of yourself so that you can live.

Fool, dreamer, bastard, he wanted to say, but that wasn't
right either. It was merely what life had given him.

He crossed the great hall, tombstone-pavers underfoot.

He watched himself, blood streaming from his cracked
skull, the essence of Enos running its course. The shade had
fallen to his knees in front of Vorax. Shadow, with his purple
eyes, watched from one side of the throne and his pale Enos
from the other.

Kip walked forward and climbed the stairs of the dais.

He knelt beside his shade just as it fell back into his arms, eyes open and fixed to the ceiling above. A whispered exhalation left his lips and then there was silence.

I'm sorry, he thought. *Rest now.*

His body faded and was gone.

Vorax watched in horror, the gold in his eyes stabbed by spikes of black.

"You...you think to destroy me with your tricks?"

"It's no alchemy, Vorax. Or none of mine, at least. It's the thing you begged for. Life."

A shadow cut across Vorax now, a cloud over the sun.

"You wanted to know what being alive felt like. This is what it feels like, a life-entire. Every bit of it gold, merely because it existed. Every joy and sorrow, success and defeat."

"I will gut you, boy, fucking bending sick boy."

Vorax was a demon now. His hands trembled as his long fingers worked, itching to be around Kip's neck. The smoothness of his shape was replaced by a skin of black knives, all in flux. They boiled as his body fought to hold onto the golden light even as it slipped away.

He stepped towards Kip, roots of black slithering over the floor. His shadowy cloak rose behind him like wings.

Dark House itself began to change, responding to its master's pain. The white constellations turned a vivid red and began to spin. The ceiling descended, contracting around the dais. Thousands of purple eyes shone dimly through windows and walls. The Shadows were coming.

His Shadow, too, was now activated, still under Vorax's spell. He bared his teeth, his face a snarling mask as he crept forward, his back arched like a hunting lion.

"After all I've given you," Vorax said, his speech labored, "an entire world for you to play in, the grandest laboratory of all, an alchemist's dream. I gave you a well to weep into, to pour your tears into. I gave you a portal to a world of raw creation, and all I asked for was one life, a life of my very own."

"No. You taught me to worship death. Death is the shadow of life."

A thousand eyes came into focus. Claws and teeth gnashed in the darkness, closing the circle around them. The black vines that came from Vorax wrapped around Kip's legs, snaked up his body, hunted for a soft spot. His hands reached for Kip's throat and found the soft muscle there.

Vorax's cold breath hit his face.

Clawed hands squeezed.

The drums boomed.

And Vorax's eyes blazed.

"I gave you a life-entire," Kip said, "including a death."

Vorax's head cracked to the side. Dark shards appeared around a hole in his ruined skull. His eyes swirled, trying to focus on Kip.

A geyser of light shot from the hole, a streaming fountain of gold that rocketed towards the ceiling. Dark House consumed it. The angry constellations returned to white as Vorax's life-force spilled into the great hall. It moved in a wave, finding every hidden corner and secret alleyway, an expanding bubble of light.

It struck the Shadows and stopped them in their tracks. The purple left their eyes. They were a silent audience now, watching and waiting.

As the bubble expanded, Dark House faded. The coldness of space gave way to a landscape of lush green. The light from Vorax's skull mingled with a rising sun, gold meeting gold. Pale London shook around them and began to collapse. Kip heard the distant rumble of stone and wood as each building fell. Towers collapsed, cobblestones cracked, and windows shattered. *Let all the fictions be erased*, he thought.

Vorax's hands fell to his sides and he stared at Kip.

The boy spoke.

"I gave you a life-entire. This one belonged to Enos and now I've given it to you. His life and his violent death. Be happy, be honored that you got to share in it."

Vorax sighed as his eyes dimmed, the last of the golden light funneled from his body. His form faded like a morning fog lifting. It moved upwards in layer after layer, unwinding black mist.

His body evaporated, like a final sigh parting from a dying man, leaving only a gray skeleton behind. The ragged collection of bones stood in front of Kip, a few bits of leathery flesh holding it together. The skeleton was malformed, curved where it should have been straight; twisting what was smooth.

The jaw hung loose, a frozen look of surprise. He wondered if this demon had gotten what he'd wanted. Had he learned the secret of life?

The skeleton tumbled forward towards Kip, clattering to the floor where it smashed to pieces. Bones spun across the marble, some slipping off the dais. A fine mist surrounded them as they turned black.

final deafening bell filled Dark House. The clock tower flared to life, shooting a column of light into the hall.

The circle of color expanded outward. Kip saw the same golden world he'd seen in his well. It was no longer contained.

It was shattered amber. Its shards moved in all directions, widening the sphere and changing everything it touched. Dark House no longer seemed such a fearsome place, and its star-scapes gave way to a palette of colors; purple and blue nebulas churning in the depths of space, the imprint of exploded stars, their light fading over the millennia.

The purest green moss sprouted between the stones of Dark House. It filled the cracks like emeralds being pushed up through the earth.

The sun climbed into the sky and washed the night away. It moved over a new landscape. Kip found it was too beautiful to process. Its images overwhelmed him as they froze in time; untouchable, incorruptible.

The bubble moved towards Enos.

Its edge washed over his colorless form and touched every cell in his body. Blood gave color to his flesh again, etching pink onto his cheeks. His eyes were as green as the moss, and twice as sharp. Kip thought of the painting over his hearth and how it had never really captured him at all, how limp and useless a thing when you could have life itself.

It was as if Enos had just woken up. He looked around, bewildered by his surroundings. The ceiling and sky moved overhead and he took it in, seeing every detail. He looked at his hands and held them up, bending his fingers as if for the first time. Then he saw Kip.

There was total silence but Kip thought that moment could have triggered an avalanche. In the past he would have swooned, or cried, or given in to any manner of self-pity, but he stood still and met his love's eyes.

Enos stepped forward and Kip met him halfway, meeting in the middle of the dais, all patterns and lines flowing out from there. This was his ship-builder and Boccherini-lover, but so much more; more than raven-haired and green-eyed, more than anything that words could bring form to.

A cloud passed over the sun and cut through the golden light, immediately vanishing everything in its path. Kip knew what it meant even if his heart rebelled.

He put a hand on Enos's cheek.

"I can't keep you," he said, and for the first time in a long time, was happy to cry. He was happy to let it come. The wall he'd hidden behind came down in tatters and he was happy to let it fall. All the passion he'd held so tightly flowed out like the tide.

"It was never my place. I kept you here," Kip said, "with my selfishness...my longing. I kept you in this in-between world. I prayed to some unholy thing, used a deeper alchemy than I should have. It was wrong, I know that, but I had to try. I thought I had to try. Go to the next place now. You're free..."

Enos leaned forward and his voice filled Kip's ear. He spoke in a mad rush, too much to say and too little time. His voice broke at times and was tinged with laughter at others. He remembered moments they'd shared and mourned the things they hadn't done. It all unwound in a stream of thought and words and it was beautiful.

"Goodbye, Kip," he said finally.

The sphere of light expanded into entropy, fading as it went. The world it created flickered like a dying candle as its light flared one last time.

In this moment of bewilderment, Kip leaned in for a kiss. He was met with warmth and breath, and the electric buzz that those things made.

A hand on the side of his face held him close, pushed a curl of red hair behind his ear. He felt the warmth of skin and the trace of every fingerprint.

"Goodbye, Enos. Goodbye, my love."

A final sigh, delicious and drawn out, filled his ears. When Kip opened his eyes, Enos was gone.

Goodbye.

29

Only stillness remained. The hundreds of Shadows stood around him in a wide circle, frozen to the spot. Their eyes were no longer purple but a pure and empty white. Kip scanned the sea of dark faces, looking for one he recognized. Would he even know his Shadow anymore?

"Shadow!" Kip called, his voice amplified by Dark House, bouncing off hidden walls, moving across the star-scape ceiling.

It faded.

Then movement.

Something roiled the sea of Shadows. The white-eyed creatures stepped aside, the crowd moving in a slow wave, and then two blue eyes appeared.

Shadow pattered forward onto the steps of the dais, his wispy black tail moving back and forth. He looked away from Kip's gaze.

"I'm...I'm sorry I tried to bite your head off."

Kip smiled. "I probably deserved it."

Shadow bounded forward, clearing the dais, and jumping into Kip's arms. Kip nearly lost his footing, but hugged his friend tightly.

There was a soft rumble and Shadow dropped from his arms and looked around the chamber. The world that Vorax had created could no longer exist without its master.

"I think we have to go out the way we came in," Kip said.

The well, he thought. Not the Pale London imposter, but the real thing, the entrance that he'd opened with his blood so long ago. He thought of the well-stones reshaping themselves to bridge the two worlds. The Pale World was a looping dream, the same drama forced to repeat itself again and again. It seemed fitting that their way out would be the way they'd come in.

Kip turned to Shadow.

"Time to go, my friend."

Shadow nodded fiercely and giggled. It was a musical sound that Kip had thought he'd never hear again.

"But how do we get back there?"

Shadow didn't seem worried, but looked at the audience that surrounded them.

"Shadows have their own kind of alchemy."

And they did.

A murmur ran through the crowd of Shadows, hundreds of white eyes activated, and focused. They looked distinct to Kip for the first time, all individuals with their own traits and character. The chattering mass of white-eyed Shadows burst to life, rising from the floor and spinning into a funnel of black. They rushed around Kip and Shadow, keeping them in the eye of the hurricane.

With Vorax gone, they were free to work their own magic.

The dizzying sea of gray sped up and tugged at them, gently pulling at Kip's clothes and hair, and then his body. He looked down as his feet left the floor, his shadow shrinking beneath him.

The dais moved away. The emerald moss that snaked across the floor had covered Vorax's bones, reclaiming each piece of his skeleton. It looked almost peaceful, soft green covering an open ribcage. A flower grew from one of his eye sockets.

It had ashen gray leaves.

Kip and Shadow ascended through the structure of Dark House, rising through columns and buttresses and beams, each interlocking piece alive with stars. They saw some inner-working there, things they couldn't comprehend.

They passed through the cathedral-like ceiling and floated over Pale London. The city was alive with its own destruction. Buildings phased in and out of sight as they crumbled, stone and wood grinding together in a contained apocalypse. Purple geysers of light shot up like venting steam. Whatever magic had held the city together was now disappearing. All the landmarks of a life undoing themselves. Each building had a history and a world of secrets folded inside it, clutching those secrets tightly as they fell.

Kip could see the ruined tower of Alchemy House, half of it already gone. The rest was collapsing. The black roof met the dark red shingles as it sheered them away, piece by piece, a butcher's knife cutting though meat.

The sights were terrifying, and the sounds deafening, but it was a joyful destruction.

Let it all turn to dust, he thought; *this world of fakery and lost dreams.*

The mass of Shadows was a dark cloud, and Kip and Shadow rode it like a carpet flying over Arabia.

They flew over the Potter's Market as a giant crack split the earth and swallowed the Three Nymphs Fountain.

The Thames boiled and evaporated into a swirling mist, exposing muddy riverbeds before, they too, dried up; hardening into dead earth.

The bridges that spanned the river buckled and writhed like serpents before falling.

Kip thought of Bonfire Night and the horrible event that had set so much in motion. Guy Fawkes got his wish after all, destroying all the constructs of the world, but it was ending in collapse, not fire.

Looking back, Kip saw Dark House still standing in the sea of rubble. It defied its surroundings. Somehow Kip knew it would remain there, only moving on its own timetable. Where it would go next, he didn't know.

They sped up, leaving the ruin of Pale London behind, and raced over the dead sea, now as still as glass. It reflected the trailing cloud they rode on as clearly as a mirror.

The world contracted as it closed around them, no longer propped up by Vorax and whatever power he'd had.

The scattered wreckage of the Library of Attila floated over the water, so much flotsam and jetsam.

The low mountain range they'd passed under flitted by as quickly as if they'd stepped over it with one long stride. Kip remembered the tunnel through it, the complete darkness and the suffocating water. And the coldness.

The dead forest with the burned Ragman tree was next, but the details were losing focus, more shapes and colors now than physical things. Soon this world would be as dark as the bottom of Kip's well again.

Lightning struck on the horizon, hitting the earth and sending maps of stars networking over the ground. Neutron stars, blue giants, supernovas, infinite drops of light massed into a swirling picture.

The wind moved in Kip's hair and filled his mouth and nostrils. Tears stung the edges of his eyes, a few dropping and flying into the distance behind him.

Shadow scanned the horizon with delight. His blue eyes filled with wonder. He put his hand on his friend's back as they watched the Pale World dim around them.

Kip didn't know if it was like waking up again, or going back to sleep, but it felt right.

A column appeared in the distance. It was the vertical expanse of his well, vanishing into the atmosphere above like a great chimney.

Its base was still there, the bridge of stones that had been their first link to this world. They were being pulled back into place, flying one-by-one to join the column of stone. As they did, the column shifted like a coiling snake.

This was the boundary for the Shadows, all but one. They spun towards the earth like diving swallows and deposited Kip and Shadow at the foot of the stone bridge. They rose into the air, swooping and diving in a great murmuration, then disappeared into the remains of the Pale World. Some went off in groups, slipping into darkness, while others flew on alone, back into the alien world.

Shadow remained and stared up at the coiling stones of the well.

"Shadow can come?" he asked, his voice quiet and unsure.

"The way I see it, I've given you something from the human world. The trade has been made, my friend."

Shadow looked down at the medal pinned to his chest and beamed.

"It sure is fancy."

Together they stepped onto the bridge of floating stones. It bobbed and shuddered beneath their feet as each stone was drawn back to the well. It took all of Kip's strength not to look down. He kept his eyes locked on the cave-like entrance, each step bringing him closer.

The world was nearly a black void now, the well-structure the only pinpoint of light. A churning sound echoed through the void. There was the sound of music in it, almost below the threshold of hearing; the beating of drums. It rolled on and on, coming in waves. Whether it sounded in his mind or in the void, Kip didn't know, but it was growing louder, driving out any thought or reason.

They scrambled into the base of the well, each stone falling away just as their feet left it. Kip struggled to gain a foothold in the column of stone that stretched above them, the smooth rocks too slippery for purchase. Shadow scampered beside him. His glowing eyes bobbed up and down as he looked back at Kip.

The interior of the well was a tower of blackness. Kip imagined the outlet, his laboratory and home; the crackling hearth and warmth waiting for him there.

The drumming came for them, ready to obliterate all remnants of the Pale World. It broke through all other sound as it stitched up the world Kip had made, his death-wish world that had to end. The drums bit at his heels.

Kip's fingers found every groove in every stone as he pulled himself up, not knowing how much more stretched above him. Shadow was next to him trying to support his body, pulling and pushing.

"I can't make it," Kip yelled above the rushing noise.

After all that had happened, he'd never planned his escape. He wasn't a magician. He had no tools to overcome this final challenge.

The stones were losing their shape, turning to a solid mist that he knew was about to break apart. Only the thinnest layer of reality still held them together.

Kip started to laugh. There was no madness in it, only surrender. It had all seemed so serious for so long that the absurdity had never occurred to him.

His laughter echoed up the well, bouncing off stone and cutting through the darkness. Shadow joined him, his soft childlike giggle adding to the echoing chorus. Kip hoped it would echo right out of the well and into London. Let laughter be the last sound he made.

Kip's muscles shook as he tried to climb one last time, the strain taking over his body. He looked into his friend's blue eyes, tracing every fleck and beautiful imperfection.

Then he let go.

The drums screamed with a fierce pounding.

Shadow jumped into Kip's arms as gravity did its work.

Together they plummeted into the decayed void of the Pale World.

A blinding crack of light stabbed Kip's eyes. It shot down the tunnel, a focused beam of energy. It etched every stone with color, illuminated them at the microscopic level.

The white light enveloped Kip and Shadow, snatching them out of the air like a reaching giant. Kip's head snapped back from the whiplash as they changed direction. His fingers brushed the tunnel wall as they sped upwards.

He could hear the electric cracking of whatever power held them. It made his hair stand on end. He imagined them rocketing through the roof of Alchemy House and into the sky above.

There was a hiccup as the air changed; some invisible boundary had been crossed. It was real air he was breathing, real sounds that filled his ears, real sights that dazzled his eyes.

Kip and Shadow sped through the circle of stone and then tumbled to an earthen floor. Kip felt the cold dirt between his fingers. It felt real and had a scent of life and decay.

A cracking sound behind him made Kip turn to see the well collapsing in on itself. The cold stone broke into jagged pieces, loud cracks filling the air. The perfect ring broke and moved like an avalanche in reverse. It knitted itself back into the ground as the light from its open mouth flickered.

Shadow was at his side now, watching. With a final *crack,* the stones crashed together and shuddered beneath the dirt floor. The light cut off, giving a final blaze before disappearing. There was a scorch mark in the dirt and a thin sliver of smoke, and then nothing but darkness.

"We're home," Kip whispered, trying to slow the beating of his heart.

A small shard of light came to life, a candle flame in the blackness, as someone approached.

"You're home," a voice said.

It was a woman's voice, both timid and strong somehow. It rode a line between two points.

As Kip's eyes adjusted he saw her face. It was pale and wore a look of injury; older than it should have been; a woman in her mid-twenties. Silver-white hair hung in her face, nearly hiding two piercing blue eyes.

It was Clover Blackmoor.

30

They sat in the living room of Alchemy House. Heavy dust covered every surface, turning the room into a soft gray landscape.

They'd beaten some of it out of the cushions of the high-backed chairs they sat in, excavating the red and yellow fabric. Clover had lit a fire in the hearth. Kip watched the fire and marveled at how real it was. He'd forgotten nearly everything except the Pale World. Memories came back to him in fits and starts, his mind seizing on one forgotten thing after another.

Most of all the fire was warm.

Clover Blackmoor put down an iron poker, rubbed her hands together, and sat in the chair next to Kip, dust billowing around her.

The question hung in the air as Kip watched her settle, now a woman grown. He didn't think he had the strength to ask it.

"Ten years," she said softly.

Shadow looked up from where he was settled, his blue eyes reflecting the fire.

Ten bells in the Pale World.

"You were gone ten years. I came to Alchemy House every day of those ten years. I looked down that well, and I waited. They wanted to take it from you, all the greedy hands in London. There were people of every kind and discipline waiting in the wings. I think I recognized their hunger, and knew Alchemy House must be yours. It was given to you, no matter how long ago, and so yours it would stay.

"I used my inherited wealth and position to keep them away, or did my best. The scavengers came none-the-less. They picked over this place."

Kip had noticed how sparse things looked. He'd forgotten what objects used to occupy the shelves, all the things he'd held so dear, things he'd almost fetishized: books, statues, candles, curios and curios.

He looked at the ceiling and saw the dead tree limbs there. They hung limply. The dark gray-green leaves had all fallen away, leaving withered branches behind.

"You can speak," Kip said.

"I could always speak. It was my father who made me mute. He began controlling me at age seven. I think I showed too much will, even then, my tongue running faster than my mind. I had more magical ability than he did and, once discovered, he had to put an end to it. I was a zombie for all those years, forced to do his bidding in silence."

Kip looked at her again and truly saw her now. Her younger self, always unreachable, had fallen away to reveal this quiet but powerful woman.

"I'm the Mistress of Magic House now," Clover continued, her voice cracking. She put her hands in her lap and knitted her fingers together. "And I have a lot to atone for; all the horrors of my father."

"No." Kip almost shouted it. He slid from his chair so that he was kneeling in front of her, and put his hands over hers. He saw the cuts on his knuckles from when he'd attacked the stone of the well when he'd first entered Vorax's underworld. They hadn't healed.

Even in ten years gone by.

"Magic does strange things," he said, "often horrible things; alchemy too, for that matter. It's the price of what we do. Your father controlled you."

"It's the price, but also the gift," she said, smiling sweetly. "I'm sorry for what my father did to you, the names he called you, the hurts he worsened. I'm sorry for the world.

"But there will be other adventures out there for you, beautiful men to match the first. There are cunning and sharp minds to know, mouths to kiss, hands to hold, a life to live."

Tears filled Kip's eyes. He let them blur his vision, let them wash the world away. They ran down his face, finding his mouth and chin, before dripping to the floor, making small circles in the dust.

Shadow purred with his deep-throated purr and pattered to Kip's side. Kip lay a hand on his head and gently stroked it.

All the tears in the world, Kip thought. *Let them come now.*

"A new start," he said, his voice cracking.

Kip told her everything. He let the story spill out breathlessly. He shared every sight and sound he'd experienced, and every emotion too. Shadow chimed in when inspired, adding to the story with his excited gestures and own perspective. Clover's attention never wavered. She nodded and listened, and asked questions when necessary.

And then it was her turn. How to sum up a decade of life? It was a neat parcel of time to work with, a block of ten years, but so much had happened. She talked of her defeats and her challenges, and how she'd emerged as the Mistress of Magic House. London had changed but had also marched on in its own untouchable way.

Kip thought of the Sulfur Glass and the visions he'd seen there.

"Did the Pale World spread out from Alchemy House?" he asked.

She nodded.

"I kept it at bay. It became another one of my daily penances when I came here, another atonement. I managed those who saw it or were affected by it, reordering their memory or erasing it altogether.

"I thought I wouldn't be able to hold it back, and perhaps I wouldn't have, but then you returned. When you came back, its power died."

She gestured to the shrunken tree limbs above.

"We'll need to clear those out," Kip said.

He looked at Clover and saw her avoiding his gaze. There was one question she hadn't asked.

"Your father died of old age," Kip said, realizing it for the first time. "Whatever magic held me down there, it didn't work for him. He...simply died of old age."

"Better than he deserved perhaps."

Even now, Kip felt some pity for the old man. He knew what it was like to be insane with desire for something you could never have. That craving could lead you forward to something better, or it could arrest and deform you.

Kip looked down to see Shadow at his side, his paws clinging to the arm of his chair.

"Kip should be doing more than catching wolves at the zoo," his friend said, his echo-voice filling the room.

Kip nodded. There was nothing else to say.

"I think you're right."

Clover rose to her feet.

"There's one last thing to show you."

Kip followed Clover.

The sights of London that he had blotted out with numbness came back to life. How vivid it all was. Each footfall possessed weight and sound, each building had texture and color. It was no longer a maze to wander in; it was his home.

Dawn approached. The sky turned a deep blue as the stars hid, whisked away by the coming sunrise.

Clover led the way. They walked in silence, but it was a comfortable silence.

They turned a corner, entering the square that led to Magic House.

Even from a distance, Kip saw the stained-glass ceiling of the dining room, now lighted up again, its colors a collection of gems.

There was something more. He could feel a new energy in the air, a palpable spark.

Then he saw it.

Dark House.

No longer a building made of stars but a real structure. It had returned to London.

It towered over Magic House like a perching raven and seemed just as watchful. The first ray of the rising sun cut across it, only illuminating its edges. It was still impenetrable. The trees that had grown in the lot while it was empty were now gathered around its edges, twisting into new shapes.

Clover spoke softly.

"There'll be many questions asked about this, but for now...isn't it marvelous?"

It is, Kip thought. Marvelous and terrible and marvelous again. It was like a battering-ram breaking through the walls of the world.

He got the sense it was looking back at them. There was no malice, just observation.

"What was it like?" Clover asked. "Inside?"

But Kip didn't know how to answer that. How could he describe it? He knew if they went inside now it would have completely changed again.

"I think it's unknowable. Maybe we'll get inside again someday. It's something you experience, not something you describe. What do you think they'll do with it?"

Clover paused.

"I think whatever power controls it, it was drawn to you when you opened the well."

"Who's its Master?"

"Surely there'll be inquests and committees, Dark House returning after a ten year absence. London will talk and fret, but I think we both know who it belongs to. You."

31

T he early morning sun streamed into Potter's Market. It painted the world with its light, gleamed off top hats, caught the silken ribbons of dresses, and the metal spokes of a carriage. All manner of customers were bathed in its glow as they flowed through the streets like water through a riverbed.

Kip and Shadow were in the middle of the crowd, sitting on the edge of the Three Nymphs Fountain. The water cut the sunlight into a thousand pieces as it streamed from the statues and landed in the pool. Kip reached down and ran his fingers over the water, breaking it into rippling circles.

The Pale World seemed like a dream, driven away by the noise and light of the real world. Had there always been this much motion? They picked up snatches of conversations, a torrent of laughter, a hushed debate, a baby's cries. If this one pin on a map was filled with so much life, imagine what the world could hold.

Endless wonders.

Kip looked down at Shadow.

"Enough is as good as a feast, don't they say that?"

Shadow nodded, "Yeah."

"This is more than enough. Maybe...maybe this *is* the feast and we have more to do and see and try. What do you think?"

"Shadow wants to do and see and try."

"Yeah, me too."

Together they found the quietest corner of the market. It was always the place with the most exotic offerings, filled with objects that were more dream than reality. These were treasures that had traveled far to get here, reaching a foreign shore just in time for Kip to look at them. Treasures that deserved the respectful silence of a museum, to be inspected with patience.

Kip spotted it first, the teetering shape of a hundred bird cages. As they approached, they found a young woman working the stand. The Bird Lady was nowhere to be found.

He remembered her kind and worried face in the Pale World, still selling her wares in the afterlife. This was the girl that had assisted her a decade ago, now fully grown. She smiled at Kip and invited him to explore the cart.

The chorus of birdsong was beautiful. They weren't shy to sing. They didn't know how to be timid or modest. *They should all be free*, he thought. *But let's start with one.*

Shadow pattered around the cart, peering into cage after cage, making little noises of discovery as he went. Kip joined him, hunting out the perfect specimen.

Tucked away behind the noise and show was a simple blackbird. While the others preened and sang, it stood in its cage, its yellow-black eye looking out at the world. The small card tied to the cage fluttered in the breeze. Kip steadied it between two fingers and read the description and smiled.

He looked down at Shadow and his friend gave a nod. Kip paid the Bird Girl and took a step away from the cart. The sun played in his eyes, casting its warmth. It was a warmth that sank into his bones and stayed there.

Offering the cage to the blue sky, he raised the small wooden gate. The blackbird didn't immediately fly, but hopped in a circle, surveying its freedom and then turning back to Kip, giving him a final inspection with one piercing eye.

Then it darted out of the cage in a blur of black. It circled the courtyard, flying past the fountain as it picked up speed. With a grace that only birds have, it darted upwards, wings flapping over rooftops. Its dark shape blended with slate tiles and twists of black smoke pouring from chimneys, before hitting the blue sky.

Up and up it went, and after that, Kip didn't know where.

ABOUT THE AUTHOR

David Pietrandrea writes urban fantasy stories set in worlds of magic and alchemy, exploring the secrets that lie just out of sight and around the corner. David is a writer, illustrator, and game developer living in Jersey City, NJ.

Author website:
    http://davidpietrandrea.com

Illustration website:
    http://www.roboxstudios.com

ALSO BY DAVID PIETRANDREA

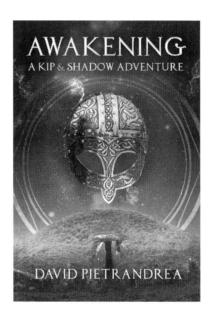

Awakening: A Kip and Shadow Adventure

Something is awake in the English countryside. The ghosts of dead warriors have besieged the town of Dorchester, terrorizing the villagers and threatening war.

Kip, and his spirit friend Shadow, are called to investigate these strange occurrences. But they've stepped into an unknown world, far from the comforts of Alchemy House and London.

Will they be able to solve the puzzle in time, or will Dorchester, and all of England, be conquered by a spectral army that wants revenge - and blood?

ACKNOWLEDGMENTS

Special thanks to the following wonderful people:

Editing and sage advice:
    Rebecca Hodgkins

Support and coffee:
    Oliver Altair
    Mike Stop Continues
    Nicole Hough
    Brian Olsen
    Sam and Dorothy Pietrandrea
    Devin T. Quin
    Josh Siegel
    Jeff Somogyi
    Michal Stocki

Made in the USA
Middletown, DE
26 June 2019